SWEET AMBER

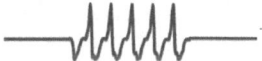

William Lynes

Black Rose Writing | Texas

First printing

This is a work of fiction. Names, characters, businesses, places, events, and
incidents are either the products of the author's imagination or used in a
fictitious manner. Any resemblance to actual persons, living or dead, or
actual events is purely coincidental.

ISBN: 978-1-68433-660-9
PUBLISHED BY BLACK ROSE WRITING
www.blackrosewriting.com

Printed in the United States of America
Suggested Retail Price (SRP) $15.95

Sweet Amber is printed in EB Garamond

*As a planet-friendly publisher, Black Rose Writing does its best to eliminate
unnecessary waste to reduce paper usage and energy costs, while never
compromising the reading experience. As a result, the final word count vs. page count
may not meet common expectations.

Praise for
SWEET AMBER

"This story will melt your heart. Is there a God in Heaven who can redeem the mess he (Lee W. Hickok, M.D.) has made of his life and the lives he encounters? Read this and find the answers along with some delightful medical case histories and entertaining personalities."
—Rebecca Farnbach, author of *Dancing With Prayers in My Feet*

"Five out of Five Stars! This book is an exemplary, fair and reasonable—This outstanding, empowering book should be given to all of our incoming First Year Medical Students both for them to read and for them to discuss with their MENTORS. Bravo Distinguished Professor William Lynes M.D.!"
—Josh Grossman, Colonel [r} U.S. Army Medical Corps, M.D., F.A.C.P.

"A medical thriller where a gifted surgeon fights his personal demons while facing accusations of misconduct. A deep look inside human addiction, whether substance or political."
—Tom Minder, author of *The House Always Wins*

"*Sweet Amber* by William Lynes provides a look into the dark side of alcohol addiction and the toll it takes on Lee W. Hickok's life. While he tackles a difficult subject, Lynes always injects humor into the day to day struggles of his characters."
—Gina Rae Mitchell, *BookSirens.com*

"Dr. Lynes has given us a compelling story; with incite and education to those not in the field; and a chilling memory for those of us who have faced that middle of the night phone call from the operating room."
—Eric J Forneret, MD

"Dr. Lynes has done it again! The thing this reader looks forward to most is his artful ability to describe each new person to the storyline. It goes without saying that the scribe leaves you wanting for his next delightful read."
—W. D. Stauffer, printer, retired

"Have you ever wondered what it might be like to be a surgeon? I recommend this story as an informative one with colorful characters and a suspenseful, engaging plot. It will touch both your mind and your heart."
—Pascal John Imperato, M.D., author of *John Pascal* novels: johnpascal,com

Patrice, thank you for your love.

SWEET AMBER

SWEET AMBER

CHAPTER 1
Operative Day

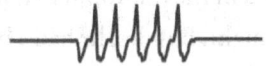

Lee W. Hickok MD locked the office door and sat with relief in his leather desk chair. Rounds were over, the clinic empty, and he was alone. He placed the basin full of ice on the desk in front of him, expecting a long night. He turned to the hidden key hanging behind his bookcase, opening the desk drawer. A ground glass tumbler and a handle sized bottle, 1.75 liter of Black Aged Jim Beam, completed the lonely triad before him. Two fingers of sweet amber poured over one finger of ice, the first sip making this hidden activity worth all the stealth in the world.

Lee W. kicked his ostrich-skinned cowboy-booted feet up onto his desk, getting comfortable. He was an alcoholic, he supposed, no down in the gutter drinker. He was a functioning alcoholic, and one who functioned well, which pleased him. Taking the relaxing second sip, he removed his surgical log from the top drawer of his desk and scanned his last one hundred surgical cases, each marked for his records by a sticky white label. Listed were the patient's name, date, and procedure, most cases completed while sipping the same beverage. Name after name passed by as he scanned. Most individuals remembered only for the procedure and a hand-written note scribbled in the margin. Yes, he functioned well, he decided, as he returned the log to the drawer.

The amber liquid had that faithful bite, as the on-call urologist sipped away. Remembering why he was present in the hospital on such a night, he reached to his in-box and re-read the memo. Dated just yesterday, a formal letter from the university hospital president reminding all on-call attendings that they must stay in the hospital, that night, New Year's eve, Friday December 31st, 1982. There was no explanation, no reason behind the break in protocol. This was a teaching hospital, the University of Texas Medical Branch (UTMB) and plenty of interns, residents, and medical students took call from the hospital, but never the attending physicians. The directive stated the expectation and left the reason to the mind of the writer.

Lee W. thought for a moment. There was something brewing in the hospital that he did not understand. Not into the politics of the institution, he did not care, though a night sleeping in his office wasn't a stirring prospect. The reason behind the directive was odd, but then the hospital president was just as odd as his name: Abbott T. Frankenstein, MD.

His last infidelity occurred in the call-room that house-staff frequented, so he was to sleep in his office that night. Besides, he had a beverage to consume. His life was lonely since his divorce, his one teen-age daughter shunning him. She was unlikely to make her way over to see him on the night before the New Year.

The basin was empty of ice when the beeper went off. Lee W. had fallen asleep in his comfortable chair, the pager vibrating away. He had a moment of disorientation as he felt in the dark, silencing the dratted device. Struggling to read the illuminated dial, he saw the extension 4696 lit in green digital numbers. Operating room two flashed in his mind from memory.

"Room two." The nurse answered on the second ring.

"This is Doctor Hickok, someone paged me?"

"Yes, Doctor Hickok. Doctor Fields wants to speak to you. Can I put you on speaker phone?"

"Okay."

"Lee W.?" It sounded as if Doctor Fields stepped away from the operating table and moved closer to the phone to speak to Lee W..

"Ya, Mark what's up?" Lee W. responded now awake.

"Got a case here that needs some U-R-O-logic attention," the surgeon said in a southern drawl. "He is a... what? A 64-year-old male that is undergoing a distal pancreatectomy for a pseudo-cyst in the tail of the pancreas. The mass involves the upper left kidney, and we got into some bleeding in the hilum that is a real nuisance. You think yaw-all could come on down and see what you can do? I would appreciate it."

"Ya, sure. You're in room two?"

"Ya, room two," Fields said, after which the phone clicked off. Regaining his thoughts after his brief sleep, he thought how odd the phone call was. In this teaching hospital, with a chief resident in urology in the house, they would not generally call the attending physician. But then maybe there was a real problem, he thought, his pulse rate picking up with some anxiety.

Downing the last amber swallow, he replaced the Jim Beam and glass tumbler in the drawer and locked it. Tossing the basin in the wastebasket he stood and grabbed his white coat hung on the inside of his office door. He moved from his office to the restroom next door. Looking at himself in the mirror as he voided, he realized that at 43 he was aging. A good looking man, tall at six foot and thin. He had piercing blue eyes and dark brown hair now tinged with grey. He had a case to do tonight, however, and as with his first case as an intern he found himself excited.

On his way to the OR, he reviewed what he knew about the pancreas. The organ lived in the center of the abdomen, its head cradled by the C shaped duodenum, and its tail lying on the upper portion of the left kidney and the center of the spleen. The pancreas makes digestive enzymes, which it excretes into the duodenum. In alcoholic pancreatitis portions of the gland dissolve, leaving what they call a pseudo-cyst. In a patient with a pancreatic pseudo-cyst abdominal pain, symptoms commonly seen include weight loss, and anorexia. Perhaps this man was a drinker, he thought as he walked.

Lee W. hit the opener for the OR doors and walked into the blaring light of what was a hectic department. Walking past the front desk, he noticed a full staff busy on the phone and fax machines. In the physician lounge several surgeons were watching financial 24 hours news, the room tousled and plain, one or two asleep on couches. He placed his white coat in his locker, took a hit on the airline size bourbon bottle, tossing it empty into the trash hamper, and redressed in a fresh green scrub suit, again surprised by the activity for a New Year's Eve.

Down the hall he walked past darkened operating rooms. When he walked into room two, he again noticed a buzz. Anesthesia stood at the head of the table with three individuals attending to details. At the table stood four gowned surgeons looking stern, the ensemble completed by the scrub nurse, conducting her table of hundreds of shiny instruments, a circulating nurse, and one man in the corner in scrubs talking on the telephone.

When he entered the room Doctor Mark Fields, chief of surgery, turned from the table and greeted him. Keeping his sterile gloved hands up and crossed over his chest, he nodded to the x-ray box on the wall behind them.

"Lee W." Fields spit out with an element of relief. "Here is his CT scan. You can see a 6 centimeter pseudo-cyst in the tail of the pancreas. It sits right over the left kidney. We mobilized the body, tail, and most of the cyst but got into some bleeding in the kidney. He has lost about five units."

"Five units?" Lee W. questioned, somewhat astonished at the volume of blood loss.

"Yes," Fields whispered, glancing for just a second at the man in the corner. "I think that left kidney will have to come out. Do you think yaw-all could scrub in and help?"

Lee W. looked at the CT scan and shook his head. "Sure," he said eyeing the left renal, or kidney vein with some attention. The cyst sat on the left kidney, the renal vein to the kidney large on the scans. "I'll have a look."

The surgeon, with a nod of thanks, glanced over his right shoulder at the unknown man using the telephone and returned to the operating table.

In the darkened hallway, Lee W. scrubbed alone. It was not his first scrub of the day, and protocol dictated therefore a five minute washing. Something about the case suggested that he should follow the teaching to the letter. So he did, first scrapping below each nail with the red plastic pick and then using the disposable brush and plenty of Betadine antiseptic soap, while watching the clock above the scrub sink.

Lee W. returned to the room, opening the swinging door by pushing with his back. This was the point he loved, entering a room of staff and physicians all there to help him resolve the situation. It was power, and the distance he had come from a small town in central Texas to this teaching institution humbled him. As he moved to the foot of the table, the scrub nurse dropped a sterile green towel over Lee W.'s extended hands. He glanced to the floor behind her. On the floor awaiting counting were over thirty blood soaked laparotomy sponges, their bloody color used to estimate blood loss. A significant number of sponges, Lee W. thought. The scrub nurse gowned and gloved the urologist after he had dried and discarded the towel in the hamper. He moved to the assistant's right side of the table and looked into the wound.

"Hi Lee W," Fields said. He reached into the middle of the operative field and said to his assistant. Keep pressure here. Under his breath he said: "bleeding like stink in here, Lee W.!" After a pause he went on. "Let me take you through the case." Using the sucker to point out the anatomy, Fields traced duodenum, head, body, and tail of the pancreas. The pseudo-cyst was a white, tense mass. It originated in the tail of the pancreas, stuck to the anterior surface of the left kidney. And then there was the spleen, full of blood and bulging, in the right upper quadrant of the abdomen.

Lee W. took the sucker from Fields. In his mind he could see two potential sources of the continued bleeding, the left renal vein or the spleen. With the sucker he retraced the anatomy, thinking to himself. The vein was somewhere behind the pseudo-cyst. It was large on the CT scan, suggesting that the cyst obstructed this vein to some extent. In addition, there was always the spleen, famous for its fragility and intra-operative bleeding.

"Does the spleen come out in a distal pancreatectomy, Mark?" Lee W. said to Fields.

"Yes, see, we have mobilized it taking down its ligaments." He said using a second sucker and pointing to the spleen's attachments to the diaphragm and the anterior left kidney.

"Is it all right to take the left Kidney, Mark?"

"Well, we hadn't planned to, but he has lost a ton of blood. I mean, if it is bleeding, it needs to go."

"How is his overall kidney function? Does he have high blood pressure?" Lee W. wondered about the result of removing one of the patient's kidneys.

"Okay to both. His creatinine is about 0.9 and he has no history of hypertension."

"Well, it would be okay to take the kidney, but let's see if we can save it. The way I see this," Lee W. said, "is that this bleeding is coming from the spleen, or more likely the left renal vein." He looked up at Fields. "The spleen, could it be bleeding?"

"No. It is all intact." He picked up the organ in his gloved hand. "What leads you to the renal vein, Lee W.?"

"Well, on that CT scan, the left renal vein is huge and there is a very large vertebral vein going into its posterior surface. We call that the vein of Leukowitz...jokingly, because this resident named Leukowitz was famous for tearing it. That the renal vein and the vertebral are so large suggests that they are obstructed, probably by the pseudo-cyst and easy to injure and hence bleed."

Lee W. now asked for a sponge stick, a long clamp with a gauze sponge on its end. With the sponge stick and the sucker, he outlined the aorta. "What we do is dissect up the anterior aorta like in renal trauma. The first vein crossing the aorta is left renal vein. We can put a vascular tape around it and look around. The bleeding will be obvious if I'm right."

And so the team turned the case over to Doctor Hickok and, using his plan, found the left renal vein. Placing a vascular tape around it allowed them to see behind the vein. Sure enough, there was a large vertebral branch, torn and bleeding. With two applied vascular clips, they controlled the vertebral vein and, the bleeding ramped down to an acceptable ooze. They left the now repaired left kidney and moved to complete the distal pancreatectomy, which occurred with no further complications.

They removed the specimen from the wound, completing the surgery. Fields looked up with relief at Lee W. With both hands, he congratulated the urologist. Several muffled claps began, as Lee W. turned from the operative field and de-gowned. He reached for the chart on the anesthesia table and retrieved a white sticky for his log in his office. Taking a moment to look for the first time at the head of the patient, he said almost to himself, "that guy looks familiar!"

Fields looked over the anesthesia barrier and said. "That's because he is your Governor, Lee W.! That's J.T. Splintter."

Lee W. just looked up with surprise. He nodded to several in the room and said. "At your service, Mr. Governor." He then tossed his gloves into the hamper and made his way out of OR two.

As he stopped to wash his hands in the OR sink, a voice over his shoulder caught his attention. "Dr. Hickok."

Lee W. turned to greet the man. It was the gentleman who had observed the case using the phone throughout. "I'm Schlomo Goldine, the Governor's chief of staff." Lee W. towered over the shorter man who stood in front of him wearing the mask not needed in the hall. He reached and shook Lee W.'s still wet hand, somewhat limply. "I don't quite understand what happened in there, but your expertise resulted in significant improvement and a successful surgery."

"Well... I can't say successful until we see how the patient does. It's too early for terms like that, but well... we lucked out. Stopped the bleeding and didn't have to sacrifice the left kidney. Yeah, I am happy with that, but successful, only time will tell."

"Well we, that is the Governor and his staff, thank you for your well-informed actions. Please come see me anytime in Austin." And with that, the man handed Lee W. Hickok a business card, and the two went their separate ways. At the entry to the OR suites, Lee W. placed his stretchy surgical hat and the now damp man's card in the trash hamper, well in view of the Governor's Chief of Staff.

CHAPTER 2
Post Operative Day Number One

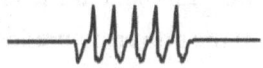

Lee W. returned to his office feeling positive. As an urologist, the solution to the bleeding was obvious, and he was thankful for his training in trauma during his residency days. He trained in Galveston, which had an active Saturday night knife and gun club. The locals, with the influence of distilled spirits, taking their disagreement out on one another. In many of those cases there was profuse bleeding, say a fracture or gunshot wound to the kidney. Here the technique that he used on the Governor, allowed the management of traumatic injuries to the kidney. With the Governor, Lee W. used this technique to identify the bleeding left renal vein.

The small vertebral vein that enters the rear of the renal vein bled, and his dissection brought him right to the vessel, jokingly called the vein of Leukowitz. Joe Leukowitz was a fellow UTMB urologist who finished his residency several years before Lee W. He was a capable enough fellow, but his attending suffered through several disruptions of that small vein during surgeries with him and coined its name. Here it was just a matter of two vascular clips and the vein stopped bleeding. This maneuver lionized the vein of Leukowitz in the Governor's surgical record. Lee W., an up-and-coming hero.

His office was pitch black when he returned. He rummaged around his white coat pocket for his keys. As he opened the door, he felt a wave of pride for a job well done that New Year's night. A much more productive night than others in the past. Most of those holidays were just expunged from his memory, with liberal doses of liquid eraser.

The clapping in the OR was a bit too much for the quiet and somewhat bashful man. That Schlomo Goldine fellow kept watching him during the case, perched over by the wall talking on the phone, giving him the creeps. But the Governor's case thrilled him.

He sat in his office chair, opened his locked drawer and poured himself a double, downed in two swallows. As he poured a second he stopped, removing the surgical log from his desk. He recovered the white sticky from his front scrub pocket. After affixing it in the log he wrote in the margin: left renal exploration, distal pancreatectomy. in parentheses he noted and underlined the patient: <u>Big Gun: Governor of Texas</u>.

So tired, Lee W.'s nerves were beginning to calm after the tense scene in the OR. The bourbon helped as well. Like an old friend, he decided. Lee W. flipped on his desk light and picked up the university president's memo from his in-box. With hindsight, he read the note again. The reason for the unusual call schedule was now obvious; there was a prominent person undergoing the knife tonight. The president wanted to impress the Governor and his staff with their minute-ready preparedness. Had the executive needed a cardiologist or a gastroenterologist or a whatever- ologist, all would be ready in a moment. Lee W. Hickok served that purpose, within minutes appearing in the OR and practicing his specialty at a phone call's whim. Was he being used? He thought for a moment, then decided not really.

At the top of the memo was its dictation date, December 30, 1982. Reading on, the memo required the attending physician on call to remain in hospital for New Year's night specified Friday, December 31, 1982. Turning to his wall mounted cuckoo clock he confirmed that it was now January 1, 1983 New Year's Day, well past the midnight hour.

Chuckling to himself, he realized that it was like he had caught his Dad in a technicality as a child. Lee W., don't climb that tree today! He could almost hear him say something like that. That daytime disclaimer would not apply to an all-encompassing tree climbing directive; he was free to climb the tree during the night or the following day. It was with logic like that that he started thinking about the rest of his evening.

He thought about his sleeping arrangement. While his office chair was comfortable, it was not the water bed he had at home. The memo had served its purpose, and he had served the Governor well. The directive brought a world class consultant at just a phone call's notice. Yes, the case continued, the man still in the hospital, now in the ICU. The Governor was general surgery's patient, however, the post-operative care the responsibility of the surgeons. Besides, it was not December 31st, but January 1st, the New Year.

He was halfway to his car when he realized he was out of his favorite Kentucky brewed Jim Beam at home. Glancing at his watch, he confirmed the obvious. It was well past the 9 pm time limit where a package or liquor store sold hard liquor in the state of Texas. Lee W. stopped walking, set his leather briefcase on the cold ground, and began tapping his cowboy footed boot with frustration. He reviewed what was available at home from memory. He had a good supply of Lone Star Beer, an ice cold case, in the basement refrigerator. Then there was the Gordon's dry Gin, Jameson triple distilled Irish Whiskey, 80 Smirnoff Vodka, Johnnie Walker Black label scotch, Jose Cuervo Tradicional tequila, and several bottles of Pedernales Texas wine, both red and white, all neatly stacked in his wet bar.

It was so disappointing, however; tonight of all nights Jim Beam would hit the spot. Lee W. decided, turned around and hurried back into the University.

The urologist took the quick back way through the central plaza of the John Sealy Hospital. Lee W. realized he had made a mistake when he rounded the corner. Flood lights were the first thing he saw, and then a small crowd, most carrying notebooks to record the details. At the podium was that man. Lee W. fought for the name, remembering the tossed wet business card in the OR trash can. Schlomo Goldine came to mind as he quietly moved up behind the small crowd.

"Yaw-all. I have an announcement about the Governor." Goldine tapped the microphone, and the crowd quieted down. Still dressed in scrubs, Lee W. thought he felt that he had completed the surgery. Standing to his left was the university president, Abbott Frankenstein. To his left was the surgeon, the chief of surgery, Mark Fields. Surrounding them were other administrators and physicians, all dressed in ties and white coats.

After the crowd died down Goldine went on. "At six pm tonight, Governor J.T. Splintter underwent surgery on the pancreas for a non-malignant pancreatic condition. Surgery was very delicate, and through all reports appears to have been very successful. The Governor is resting now in the recovery room. He is stable and will move to the intensive care unit for close monitoring soon. During this period of incapacity the Attorney General, Warren Thornton, will be in charge of administering the business for the State of Texas as the acting Governor.

Lee W. started inching off at the rear of the crowd. He turned around and was about to head to his office when he heard his name.

"Dr. Hickok assisted at that point, and we appreciated his expertise. Dr. Hickok is, well, he is right there." He said pointing to Lee W. Now the entire room focused on him. He shook his head and continued to smile.

"Would you care to answer a question or two, Doctor Hickok?" Schlomo Goldine now had the microphone and was waving for the doctor to come to the stage. Doctor Mark Fields was smiling like a gator and began a quiet clap for the man. Lee W. had no choice; he picked his way forward to the makeshift stage.

The first question came from a female reporter from KTRK in Houston. "Doctor, what was your role in the operating theatre?"

Lee W. looked at Fields, who nodded.

"This procedure often involves the kidneys. The kidney is my area of expertise... I am an urologist. There was some very mild bleeding from the left kidney and we as a team could address that, and the bleeding resolved."

"Did you remove the kidney, Doctor Hickok?" Another reporter asked.

"No, we did not."

"Doctor, what causes his pancreatic disease?"

Lee W. was silent. He turned and glanced at Doctor Frankenstein, who stepped forward and took the microphone. "Governor Splintter had developed a pancreatic pseudo-cyst which was causing severe abdominal pain and poor eating."

"Is Governor Splintter an alcoholic?" Said a reporter from the crowd.

Schlomo Goldine stepped up to the mike and answered. "Documentation shows that the Governor is only a social drinker. With that, we will end this update. We will be available sometime tomorrow afternoon for further updates."

Lee W. could not get off the stage soon enough. He grabbed his briefcase and headed toward his office. On the way he met Mollie, the OR scrub nurse. She had a huge smile on her face as she embraced the urologist. "Yaw-all is the man, Doctor Hickok."

"Don't say that Mollie, I just did what I had to do."

"No... it was a mess in there before you came in. After you did what you did, the bleeding stopped outright it did. Did you see them bloody sponges on the floor? The man was bleeding to death!"

Lee W. shook his head. He thanked the woman, gave her a hug, and then hurried down the hall entering his urology clinic.

He opened the door to his office, made it to his desk drawer and removed the bottle of Jim Beam. Holding it up against the light through his outdoor curtains he estimated that 1/3 of the bottle remained. Thinking this was better than nothing, he put the bottle in his open topped leather briefcase. Sitting up, the snout of the large bottle just stuck out of the flap.

He made his way to his car, bypassing the fiasco in the hospital central plaza with no one seeing him. Opening the door of his newly painted Datsun 240Z, Lee W. placed the briefcase on the passenger seat. The urologist secured his seat belt, pulled the manual choke and started the car, turning on the driver's seat warmer switch in the console, making sure it was off on the passenger side under his favorite beverage. Lee W. flipped on the AM/FM radio playing the top hits of 1982.

He shifted through the manual transmission, making his way down Seventh Street toward Seawall, turning right on that thoroughfare. To his left was the Gulf of Mexico, waves crashing with the usual tropical storm brewing. The police lights were in his rearview mirror before he had gone a block. He pulled over with anxiety, wondering what he could have done, popping a breath lozenge into his mouth.

The officer pulled up behind him, leaving his lights twirling in the chilly night air. Lee W. watched him in the rearview mirror as he opened the driver side door, the big man walking up on his left. When he reached his car Lee W. had already dropped his window and retrieved his license. Not only could he see the sea but now he heard the waves crash to *Every Breath I Take* by the band the Police, a possible premonition for his future.

Handing him his license, Lee W. reached over and opened the glove box removing his registration. As he did so he noticed the neck of the Jim Beam bottle sticking out of his black leather briefcase like a signpost. He sucked on his breath lozenge and swallowed hard. Did he really need the Jim Beam tonight, he wondered?

Returning to the officer he handed the registration to the man. Thinking about his passenger, he couldn't make eye contact, studying instead the officer's badge reading the golden embossed name of Lieutenant Willie Washington.

Officer Washington studied the registration in silence. As he scanned the document he asked: "do you know why I stopped you tonight, Mr. Lee Hickok?"

Lee W. licked his now dry lips. He whispered, wondering if his beverage raised an odor. "No officer, I know I wasn't speeding."

Still reading the registration with his head down, the officer said: "Taillight is out."

With some relief, Lee W. heard the officer answer, still inspecting the registration.

"This here a nineteen and seventy-two 240 Z?" The officer said somewhat to Lee W.'s relief.

"Yes, Officer."

"This sure is a nice green color," he said, touching the green metallic door's edge. He paused for a moment, looking at the car's console. "What's that switch there?" He said pointing to the shifter console mounted seat warmer switch.

"What... what do you mean?"

"That switch," he said bending down and pointing a huge hand into the car indicating the switch behind the shifter, next to the driver's seat.

"Well, it turns on the seat heater."

"What about that switch?" He said pointing to the switch next to the passenger seat and the briefcase. Before Lee W. could answer the man reached up across his body and pulled the Jim Beam bottle up by its snout. Examining the bottle in the light outside of the car, the man sighed and bit his lip. He reached back across Lee W. and placed the bottle on the passenger seat.

There was some sadness in Willie Washington's voice as he asked Lee W.: "Have yaw-all been drinking tonight, sir?"

Lee W. hesitated. Eventually he lied. "No sir, I brought that bottle home from the university."

"But that bottle is open, is it not?"

"Yes. Yes it is officer."

"I'm afraid I will have to ask you to get out of the car."

Lee W. looked out the front windshield with anxiety. Frost accumulated on the window, obscuring his vision, the cloudy windshield similar to his predicament. He unlocked and opened the door.

"Officer I was just on my way home." He stretched the truth as his house was quite a ways away. "I live just blocks down Seawall." He pointed east down the Gulf lined thoroughfare.

"1077 63rd Street. I know," he said, placing the registration and driver's license under the clasp of his clipboard after pulling out a white Xeroxed sheet. Looking down the Seawall he said: "Quite a few blocks, right near six lights, I'd say." As he slipped the sheet under the clasp.

Listening again to the roar of the surf, Lee W. looked down at his cowboy boots in despair. He realized he was in trouble.

· · ·

Lt. Willie Washington had spent an quiet New Year's Eve night on patrol. He broke up a fight at the Galvez Hotel, 19th and Seawall, and beyond an arrest after a knife fight on the Strand, his night had been boring. When he saw the man with the taillight infraction he loss concern for the the faulty running gear, but his interest centered on the beautiful car. The man was driving a to-die-for Datsun

240 Z, and he knew immediately that he would write him a fix-it ticket. A brief yelp from his siren, and the man pulled promptly to the side of the road. He had his window down when Willie approached. As he stood waiting for his documents, the Retsyn containing Cert breath mint wrapper on the console grabbed his attention. His father carried them continuously, the same Certs Cool Mint Drops brand and flavor used to hide a Dixie Beer case-a-day addiction smelling breath.

His specialty then kicked in. Traffic stops for driving while intoxicated, DWI in Texas, were cat and mouse games between the officer and perp, or suspect. Sometimes the intoxication was obvious, sure there were some cases where the perp fell out of the car, but often the chronic drinker did pretty well on field sobriety tests. The game that he enjoyed so much was first, picking up on the intoxication and then second, nailing the blood alcohol level when they administered the breath analyzer test done at the detention center. Those educated guesses were teased from the entire contact with the perp and compared to hundreds of past suspects.

The breath mint was the first sign in favor of intoxication. He thought in his mind as he reviewed the registration, looking out of the corner of his eye to the interior of the sports car. He used his mentor Sammy Townsend's trick; find something to comment on inside the vehicle and then use that to look around for an open container. Here, the switch on the car's console was interesting to the auto buff. Seat warmers; he didn't know Datsun, like Mercedes, had such comforts. After he questioned him about the switch he had a reason to reach into the car. Then it was so obvious. Right in the black leather satchel sitting upright on the passenger seat was the key to the arrest, a partially consumed bottle of expensive whiskey. The finding gave reason for asking the man to step out of the car and administer field sobriety testing.

The game was on, guess his blood alcohol level (BAL). The perp opened the car door and exited to stand smooth enough. He avoided eye contact, however, looking down at his boots; a subtle sign of something to hide. When the officer explained that he was completing a Drug Influence Report he continued to stare at his feet as if the Ostrich skinned boots were worth their weight in Texas oil. Completing the form, Washington found his speech non-slurred, attitude cooperative, breath minty mixed with alcohol, mild blood-shot eyes, and coordination, okay.

"What do you do for a living, Mr. Hickok?"

"An urologist, a surgeon," Hickok said, again dropping his eyes to his boots. Coordinated enough to perform surgery, the officer wondered how it would affect the field sobriety test.

Horizontal gaze nystagmus, the rhythmic beating of the eyes when deviated, was present in his left and right eyes at 35 degrees. On Rhomberg testing, asking the man to stand on one foot with arms extended at his side and lean back his head for 30 seconds, the perp lasted just 15 and then leaned but only slightly to his left. There was a normal convergence in both pupils when he asked to stare at his approaching index finger. When asked to walk boot to boot for 9 steps forward and backward Hickok made it five steps forward and then gave up on the task.

So Lt. Washington had his data, which he summarized to himself while talking to the man. The taillight gave him probable cause to stop the vehicle, right taillight non-functional. His visual inspection revealed an open alcohol container. His field sobriety test showed some subtle signs; watery blood-shot eyes, minty alcohol tinged breath. In addition, his field test showed some lack of coordination, horizontal gauze nystagmus, a positive Rhomberg test and faulty foot to foot walking. The officer suspected driving while intoxicated, and he calculated in his mind his guess at BAL: 0.18.

"You know I will have to arrest you, Doc." The officer said as he slipped behind the perp. "Place your hands behind you," he said as he cuffed Lee W., the click of the cuffs a death like omen as he accompanied the perp to his car.

• • •

Hickok bit his lip as he sat in the officer's black and white Chevrolet Malibu. He swallowed the dissolved breath mint, the worthless candy burning as it dropped along his dried palate. From a physician minding his business in his office, to hero, now to perpetrator with an open alcohol container and driving while intoxicated, his day had been a roller coaster. He just wanted to get back to practicing urology, something he would find troublesome in the coming days.

CHAPTER 3

Post Operative Day Number Two

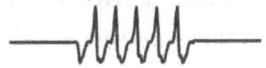

Stopped for the suspicion of drunken driving before, but never arrested before. However, this soiree in jail was not the first for Lee W., just the most painful. He remembered being a child of eleven when, for fright's sake, he had spent some time in the Katy, Texas, jail.

His neighbor, Billy Jr., had a backyard full of old cars, rusting out in the central Texas heat. The 1956 faded two tone turquoise, De Soto Firedome, hardtop with the stylized hood ornament of Hernando de Soto had always caught his juvenile mind. He noticed the safety glass label in the windshield's corner when examining it one summer day. Attempting to smash it in with an old roofing hammer testing its safety proclamation seemed to follow. He had just learned that safety glass was in fact unbreakable, when Billy Jr's elderly, and outright frightening, grey-haired grandma appeared out of the backyard screen door. Her scream was worse than the sound from the blow he had just administered, her reaction like he had just bashed the presidential limousine. She had her shoe off in a blink, and nailed him upside the head, dazing him like a helmet to helmet tackle in the NFL. She had him by the ear before he could run. Unlucky for Lee W., Billy Jr's Dad's Texas Rangers shift was just beginning, and the woman had him in the back seat of his cruiser in a speed defying her fifty-ish age. The time spent in that car and back at the precinct where the Dad, Lee W. assumed Billy Sr., gave him an Eskimo pie, may have contributed to his future life free from crime. Now ratchet forward some 30 years and he wished that episode had protected him from a DWI.

His night woes began in the back of Lieutenant Willie Washington's Chevrolet police vehicle, where he learned that sitting on a hard bench back seat while handcuffed behind your back was uncomfortable. At the police station he sat and sat in that air-conditioned freezing vehicle until the officer ushered him in. Time then seemed to stand still within the precinct. When they administered the expected breathalyzer test, the officer seemed almost giddy with the result, 0.18, as if he had won a lottery.

While booked, fun continued. He stood for the longest time at a narrow window until an overweight woman with persistent acne plastered over with what looked like *Bisquick* make-up, asked him a series of questions, all asked before. He had Miranda rights read but without the flare and excitement of Hawaii-5-O. Asked then to strip in the property room, they placed each item of clothes into his own personal brown paper bag. He arrived in the intox cell where his only roommate kept asking all night for *skinny girl,* which he learned was cocaine.

The phone call was something that Lee W. did not look forward to. As he sat in the intox cell, his mind roamed through his few potential contacts. He could call no one from the university. It was Sunday, and his lawyer who handled his divorce left just a taped message. Afraid that this was his last call, relief came when they told him to dial another person.

Amber was his ex-wife. She was a fine enough woman, but right now she hated Lee W. She called him, a drunk so often that he did not hear the disparaging remark anymore. His phone call, so early Sunday morning, did nothing to change her opinion of the man.

Standing at the pay phone, Lee W. dialed the number from memory with severe reluctance. As the telephone rang, he read the graffiti laden wall. *For a good time call Delilah N Axe for the double treatment,* and so on.

"Hello?" The sweet little voice called out just awakening from a dream filled sleep.

Lee W. remembered how precious the woman was when she was sleeping, but quickly realized her other side from years of marriage. "Amber?"

"Who is this?" The woman now awake and aware of something unpleasant.

Wasting no time, he asked the question. "It's Lee W. I need you to pick me up at the police station."

"Oh... not you. And what time is it?"

"Hell if I know I'm arrested."

Her other side emerged. That side was defensive and developed during the later years of their marriage. She was disappointed, what with one case of infidelity, massive drinking and years of disillusionment. She spoke in her voice of self-protection. "You horse's ass, and you call me?"

"Listen, I got no one else to call. My car is in impound, I just need a ride across town to get it."

"And you thought you could call me. Oh... oh... this is perfect. Lee W. needs help. And just what is the good doctor in jail for? Pickup an undercover officer whore and propositioned her? No, you're too impotent for that." And then she guessed. "Wait a minute. I know. Yaw-all got stopped for drunk driving, didn't ya!" All said with a now awake viral laugh.

"Yes... I mean... a DWI."

Someone tapped on the wall behind Lee W. He was taking too long with his phone call. "Come on Amber, I just need a ride. I wouldn't ask, but I am desperate."

"Oh yes. Yaw-all's desperate if you call me."

Amber yelled in response to someone asking who it was on the phone. "It's okay Kellie, it's just your deadbeat Dad who got himself arrested for, are you surprised, drunk driving!"

"Don't tell her that!"

"You think a 15-year-old won't figure it out. Hell, you fell over face down in the mud at her first softball game. Remember that Lee W.!"

"Amber." He said, remembering only being told of the blacked out incident.

The man waiting for the phone behind him was yelling now. "*Yaw-all gets off da phone before I bus yer ass, jack.*" He punctuated his threat with a kick to the floor board below the phone.

So Amber with reluctance agreed to pick up Lee W. and transport him across town to the impound. He waited for what seemed hours. As usual, she took her appearance seriously. She appeared as a MTV diva, strutting a sexual stride best suited for the finest music video. Her perfect face and lioness green eyes were framed with thick, wind-blown blonde curls that cascaded down a black studded leather jacket worn over high-water green pants and black, high-heeled pumps. Officers stood to take notice of the beautiful woman who entered the precinct and asked for Lee W. Hickok in her sweat girlish tone of voice. Relief came over him, when they buzzed him out of lockup. Standing there with his brown paper bag and looking at his beautiful ex-wife he felt just a modicum of understanding and so he hugged the woman superficially. She refused his embrace, just shook her head, and the two headed out. Once outside in her car the two sat and stared ahead. Amber then fired up the car, and they drove in silence, parking in front of the impound.

Amber was the first to speak. "Well, there yaw-all go, Lee W." Turning in her seat she found a position to look the man in the eyes. With surprising sincerity she said: "You need to stop drinking Lee W." Her next sentence was surprising. "Honey, don't yaw-all think it's time?"

"I know." Lee W. said with true seriousness, dropping his head to break eye contact. "Been thinking about that all night." He said as he unlocked the passenger door and lifted himself out. Amber drove away as Lee W. was closing the car door. He stood looking longingly at his ex, as she scattered dust behind her.

Lee W. inspected every inch of his prized 240Z in horror. During the impound they had keyed the left door, the sign of superman perfectly centered below the driver's door handle. The car was a mess, as if someone had driven it around and around in the dirt lot. It came caked with mud on the Italian Pirelli tires, the radio antennae broken off, and there was an unexplained crack in the front windshield. As expected, the personalized license plates, NUTDOC, were missing.

He opened his personal brown paper bag and found his keys. He was home in his driveway in just a few minutes, driving slowly and obeying all the street signs and laws known or imagined.

Lee W. would have loved to park in the detached garage, but it was full, as was most of the house, now packed with restoration supplies. The urologist lived in a Victorian house on 63rd Street. His plan was to fix up the old home and restore it to its turn of the century beauty. The restoration was going slowly, Lee W. doing most of the work on a haphazard schedule. The problem was money and time, what with alimony on an assistant professor's salary, and the time constraints of practicing medicine. Now he did not know what would happen, what with his DWI.

When he looked in his liquor cabinet, he missed his beloved Jim Beam. Confiscated for evidence, the bourbon's absence was disappointing. He poured himself a shot of the second choice, Johnnie Walker Black label, and downed it without thinking. Taking the bottle with him, he climbed the stairs and plopped down in his waterbed. It reminded him of the night's crashing gulf, as he dropped off into deep sleep.

The phone woke him up in a startled state. Lee W. still had his pants on, one cowboy boot, his head hanging over the waterbed. His hair stood on end, his beard now Miami Vice stubble, what without a razor going on two days. Someone had finished the near full bottle of Johnnie Walker. While he supposed it must be him, he had no memory of it.

He looked at his alarm clock which announced the day and time: Sunday 3:04 pm. The phone continued to ring, as Lee W. figured that it was still the weekend and therefore still on call.

"Hello."

"Is this Professor Lee W. Hickok?" Said a voice on the phone.

"Yes..." Lee W. answered, thinking of his recent arrest.

"Congrats professor!"

Lee W. recognized the voice. "John, what do you mean?" John Cooper was the chief resident in urology at UTMB.

"You're a hero, man. The vein of Leukowitz? You told the surgeons about that?"

Lee W. was still half asleep, as his mind traced back to what Cooper was talking about. It seemed a year away, somewhere in someone else's life. However, yes, at the university he was somewhat of a hero, but in his mind he was something else.

"What's up John?" Lee W. wondered, knowing that a phone call from housestaff meant work. He realized as well, that the university did not know about his recent legal troubles.

"Well, I have a case to discuss with our hero." There was the catch; he figured he would soon be back in the operating room. The thought gave him some sense of personal accomplishment and pride, something he was not feeling up to now.

"What's going on?"

"There is a 28-year-old male that Thompson saw in our world famous establishment. Three days ago, he gives a history of hearing a popping sound during masturbation while high on PCP." Thompson Smith was the resident on call in the house or hospital. He had seen a patient and called the chief resident, and the chief resident called the attending Lee W. Something like the military's chain of command.

"Three days ago?"

"Ya, the dirt bag was too high to come in. He didn't have much pain either, that is until he tried beating off again this morning. Probably ran out of PCP. He is still real swollen and bruised at the base of the penis. Really, gives a great history of penile fracture."

"Ya, but three days, don't think we can do much. He needs a corporagram."

"Did one. Shows extravasation at the right base." Cooper did an x-ray with dye injected into the meat of the penis. This was an injury that occurred to the penis only when erect. The force of, in this case masturbating, tears the penis allowing high pressure blood to escape into the surrounding tissues.

"Then we should explore him, John."

"Already on the way to the OR, could you scrub in Mr. vein of Leukowitz hero?"

Getting out of bed and dressed was hard for Lee W. It was the damn Scotch, he rationalized. Remembering the loss of his precious Jim Beam, he rationalized that he *tolerated that liquor* so much better. After shaving and showering, he wandered into his half- finished kitchen and made a quick pot of coffee. After adding a generous dose of brandy, he was out the door and on the road to UTMB, a breath mint in his mouth.

In the OR was a wall to wall banner announcing: Texas' Operating Room of Choice. Someone had drawn a very good caricature of Lee W. in the corner with a black grease pencil. In the OR it turned out that he was a hero. Nurses, surgeons, anesthesiologists, nurse anesthetists all congratulated him. It embarrassed Lee W. at first, but soon he took in the adulation, forgetting his recent run-in with the law.

The case was straightforward. They repaired the fractured area of the penis and left a drain to dra*in a*ny drainage.

In the recovery room nurses continued to congratulate Lee W. It turned out in retrospect that the staff liked and respected the urologist, despite knowing that he drank like a fish. It never affected his practice, and rumors of this did nothing but ingratiate him in the mind of the Texas medical staff. In reality, people, nurses, liked the man. Had they only known what a turnaround that was.

During his internship, they called him in for an evaluation on his first general surgery rotation. He was told that he was the best intern the attending had seen, hardworking and thorough, but the nurses hated him. Lee W. realized at the time that yelling and lambasting the staff made his life as a housestaff so much harder. He vowed at the time to change, and do so he did, turning around his hospital wide impression. In the coming days the hospital's staff would have to comment on the urologist's performance. He did not realize how much this groundwork would benefit him.

CHAPTER 4
Post Operative Day Number Three

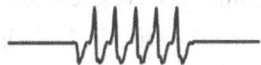

Another banner heralded his hospital arrival the next morning. It announced the hospital's pride, this time his caricature printed directly onto the ten foot paper placard. Zealously inscribed was Texas' Hospital of Choice- UTMB, in the University of Texas orange and white letters. It turned out that the hospital was replete with similar signs and posters, as the medical branch self-celebrated the Governor's choice of medical institution and his *successful* surgery. Lee W. looked at the banner with some skepticism, clinging to his statement the night of surgery that successful would take time to determine. He felt an ominous feeling. Would this over done celebration haunt him?

He opened the door of his office, after thanking the staff in the urology clinic for their platitudes. Lee W. tore down the poster with Texas' choice and his caricature taped to the bookcase, now with some anger, and tossed it in the trash can. The urologist closed the partially open curtains and turned on the light. He had another handle sized Jim Beam bottle in his trusty briefcase, this time turned on its side to conceal it. Removing it, he opened the locked drawer and removed the glass tumbler. A finger shot of amber was downed, after which he returned the sweet amber to the locked drawer.

Lee W. sat in his leather chair and reviewed his life situation with some anxiety. He made a note to call his lawyer, Andrew Calhoun. The urlogist felt certain that the DWI would resolve, for this was his first violation. Lee W. predicted a simple slap on the hand with minor law proceedings. Lee W. was a law-abiding Texan; he had not even ever had a traffic ticket. Yes, he would contact Andrew Calhoun today. It was just a precaution however, just covering himself.

His mind then turned to his ex-wife, Amber. He thought of the beautiful woman, driving away and leaving him in the dust of the impound. Over the years, their relationship had been a violent and tumultuous one. He could not help himself, however, he still loved the woman. Even after three years post-divorce he hoped, perhaps irrationally, for reconciliation. He put on his desk calendar a reminder; he would call the woman, put up with her sarcasm, and thank her for her help. Maybe he could even ask her to dinner. Amber loved Luigi's Ristorante Italiano on the Strand, the historical district in Galveston. With a good bottle of wine and Lobster Ravioli, perhaps he could get back on her best side.

He then vowed to not be distracted by this hospital hysteria. The attention was unwarranted and worried him. Lee W. knew that he had done what any good urologist would have done. He realized that he had a large proportion of good luck that night. Lee W. read the CT scan, seeing the swollen renal vein. The man put two and two together and lucky for him they equaled four; the vertebral vein was bleeding.

After retrieving a hot cup of coffee, he poured a shot of sweet amber into his personalized UTMB Mug. Feeling a little better after planning out his day, Lee W. stood and reached for his white coat. He now found himself ready to get back to work, first round with the residents and then work another busy clinic day. He picked up the phone and paged John Cooper.

"Ya boss," The Chief resident responded answering the page.

"How'd our case do last night? What's his name, McNulty?"

"Ya... Oh, you know what. She is so funny! Karen Green, the intern, calls him McNUTTY." Lee W. said referring to the penile fracture case of the prior day. "He did all right. He drained minimal out of his Jackson Pratt." Referring to minimal drainage from the suction drain placed at surgery. "We got him up out of bed walking in the hallway today. When do you want to take out the drain?"

"Soon, if he is not draining, and then he can go home. John, I was thinking about making quick rounds. Could you meet me on the ward?"

"Ya sure, I got a half hour till the OR starts up. I'll grab the Stream Team and meet you."

· · ·

The urology ward was in the *old* John Sealy Hospital. John Sealy Hospital opened in 1890 as part of the University of Texas Medical Branch, the first medical school west of the Mississippi. The widow and brother of one of the richest citizens of Texas, John Sealy, founded the hospital after the man's death. A second John Sealy Hospital followed in 1954 to replace the 1890 building. In 1978 they completed the current or *New* John Sealy Hospital, standing on open land just next to the 1954 facility. At this point in history, then the *old* John Sealy was the 1954 facility. Housed in this older facility, primarily containing open type multiple patient wards, were the urology patients.

The entourage gathered in the urology ward nursing station. Five white coated individuals were talking, waiting for their attending physician, Lee W. to arrive. They included John Cooper the chief resident, Thompson Smith the urology resident, Karen Green the surgery intern, and two medical students.

They could not help but overhear the ward clerk's discussion. Everyone called her Miss Bonnie, the woman employed at UTMB longer than anyone could remember. She was an African-American woman, thin with straightened black hair pulled back in a bun, and mile long curved, painted fingernails, She was someone you should not cross. She was talking to a nurse's aide, Mrs. Allen, a hefty black woman as round as two of the bedpans she carried.

"Mrs. Allen... there's an order here for yaw-all." Miss Bonnie handed the nursing aide the flagged hospital chart. "He's that man from yesterday, yaw-all know... the one with the broken dingdong. Oh... that one hurts, it does. How do yaw-all break a penis anyhow?" The ward clerk looked up at Mrs. Allen seriously, hoping for some education. When the aid answered only with a silent smile, Miss Bonnie answered for herself. "Well, he must a broke that there gristle inside. Ouch... right on top of the bone. I know he-shamed. Does he have a cast?" The ward clerk wondered now, laughing to herself.

The nursing aid answered, "Say what? No, he don't," shaking her head, as she took the chart to note the new orders.

Lee W. arrived as the group began laughing. He dressed in a white coat, light blue button-down collar shirt with a red and navy blue tie. Black trousers over a dark brown pair of well polished Buffalo hide cowboy boots completed his attire. The group turned to their leader, covering up what they were laughing at.

Lee W. wondered about the joke. When Cooper explained what Bonnie had said he laughed much stronger than he had in the last 48 hours. Then he turned to the nursing station wall, where another of those banners was hanging. With mild anger, the man looked to the sky with exasperation. The entire group was now surrounding him.

Lee W. asked the intern quietly. "Karen, look into getting that banner removed today!" With enthusiasm, the girl looked down at her scut-work laden clipboard and scribbled one more of what looked like a hundred things for her to do today. The group then moved to the end of the ward, with the medical students pushing a wire wheel basket containing each of their patient's charts.

Karen stepped up at the first bed, the group filing around her. "Mr. Olds is a 59-year-old man now in post-op day #2 after radical prostatectomy. He has been afebrile, tolerating liquids well and has put out 25 cc from his right and 50 cc from his left Jackson Pratt drains." The intern presented the first patient as a man after a prostate resection for cancer, who had not had a fever, and had drained the specified amounts from his pelvic drains in the last 24 hours.

Cooper said: "He is not walking well. We will kick his butt out of bed today," the chief resident added to the attending. After open surgery, ambulation is a life preserving action, used to prevent pneumonias and blood clots. It was rough, but the hospital staff had to encourage walking, which because of the incision was very painful. "I thought we could DC the right JP today and the left tomorrow if okay." Here the reference was to removing the right drain and if no problems the left the next day.

All members of the team looked at Lee W., who shook his head in agreement. "Ya, that's good. Let me see your ears, Karen." Lee W. stretched out his hand and the intern handed him her pink stethoscope with a little Olivia pig doll sitting between the two ear tubes. Moving to the bedside, he pulled the curtain for privacy. "Mr. Olds. How yaw-all this morning?"

Before the man would speak he reached into his bedside drawer and placed his dentures in his mouth. "Doc, I hurt real bad, and them all want me to walk!" He said waving the back of his IV containing hand at the group. "What am I supposed to do?"

Lee W. said nothing, but gently had the man sit forward in bed, about to make a teaching point that he was famous for. "Take a deep breath," he said, as he put the stethoscope to back of the patient's chest. After two poor inspirations, Lee W. handed the scope back to the intern. He shook his head. "Look, Mr. Olds. You're just about to catch pneumonia. It is very important for you to get moving."

"But I hurt Doc! This incision down here," he said, pointing to his lower abdomen covered with a paper taped dressing. "It hurts just to cough!"

"Well I understand, but I can hear a pneumonia just beginning to breed down in your lungs. Yaw-all got to get moving. Here's what you do, Sir," Lee W. said with respect. He turned to Karen and asked: "Yaw-all got morphine ordered still?"

Karen shook her head.

"How much?" He said.

"Eight to ten milligrams IM every four to six hours prn pain." Karen said without needing to review the chart the medical student was just retrieving.

"Okay," Lee W. said. "First, yaw-all up that to every three to four hours. What we'll do for you Mr. Olds is give you a larger dose. So he gets the ten milligrams." He said looking at the intern. Turning again to the patient, he went on. "I want yaw-all to take a shot. Then wait one hour till that med is working in your veins. I want the nurses to help you get just to sitting in the chair. After lunch, take another pain shot, wait an hour, and then the nurses can get yaw-all walking to the door. That way each time you have your pain shot yaw-all go just a little further. Do you think you can do that, Mr. Olds?"

"Will that cut the pain, Doctor Hickok?" The patient asked while he clicked up his falling denture.

"Yes, it will. Yaw-all take a shot and then get moving in one hour. Then do the same thing but walk to the door after lunch. After dinner you can walk in the hall."

"Yes, I will do that. But the food is awful!"

"What meal type yaw-all got him on?" Lee W. wondered, turning to the group.

"Clear liquids." Karen responded.

"Ya that stinks real salty. He got bowel sounds?" Lee W. wondered if the man had sounds upon auscultation of his abdomen.

"A few."

"Give him a regular diet." Lee W. now put his hand on the shoulder of the man. "But go slow now. Don't yaw-all go chowing down and get to vomiting."

"Okay Doc."

The group moved from bed to bed. "That pneumonia trick gets them moving every time." Lee W. said as he gave himself a new breath mint. Karen presented each patient to the group, the chart supplied if needed by the medical students. Lee W. would then slowly add something here and there teaching them the art of bedside manner and a few tricks to gathering the patient's confidence.

John Cooper silenced his pager. "It's room four. I got a TURP to do." Here Cooper was talking about doing a transurethral resection of the prostate, a prostate resection through the penis for voiding problems. Often done by the resident, the chief resident was taking the case.

"A TURP? Isn't Thompson doing that?" Lee W. wondered. He looked around and found Thompson looking down at his boots, somewhat unhappy with his superior's decision.

"Got to get my hundred TURP's before I finish!" Cooper said, referring to the dictum that a resident in urology should do 100 TURP's before graduation.

"Okay." Lee W. said. "We are just about done. But where is our penile fracture?"

"He's in the single room." Thompson Smith answered.

Lee W. twisted his head curiously. "What problem brought that case to the solitary room?" In the now ancient 1954 hospital, most patients were housed in large wards, the beds separated by curtains. On each ward there were one or two private rooms that could be used as needed.

"He is difficult to take care of."

"Okay, you John go on to the OR. We'll look at McNutty... I mean McNulty. Look at what yaw-all have me doing. Do we have anyone in the ICU?" Lee W. wondered.

As Cooper was leaving he answered "No...," but then stopped with a big smile on his face! "What am I saying? J. T. Splintter. The Governor your hero-ness."

Lee W. indicated that they would see McNulty. He wondered whether he should visit the Governor, who now in POD #3 was still in the ICU.

The group made their way past the nursing station and stopped in front of the door to the private room. Here Thompson Smith took over the job of presentation. This patient is Michael McNutty... I mean McNulty. Quiet chuckles were heard; Thompson let the silence magnify it. "He is a 28-year-old PCP addict in POD#1 after penile exploration, and repair of corporal fraction. He had a wild night. The guy drove me crazy! I was called all night about this guy with complaints of pain, anxiety, visions, to wanting to chew gum, to his needing to masturbate. Can you believe that! I had to come down from the call room on that last request. Caught him working his member, wasn't able to get an erection though. It terrified him; I had to calm him down with some IV valium. Thinks he will never get to use that boy again. That's when we moved him into the single room. His exam looks good. Minimal bruising. He had 10 cc out of his JP drain."

They entered the room to see a young beach type with shaggy brown hair and large earrings in both earlobes, dressed in a hospital gown and sandals. He was attempting to void into a urinal, his naked back exposed to the entire team. When done voiding, he hung a yellow filled urinal on the bedrail, gingerly moved and sat down in his bed. Right away he began starring and smiling strangely at the female intern, Karen Green.

"Glad to see you voided, Mr... Mc... Mr. McNulty?" Thompson asked, holding in a laugh with restraint, trying to say the man's name.

"Ya I want out of this joint. Who's the captain? All night I see strangers in my room. But I need some strong pain meds!" The patient said, looking from one individual to another.

"We have Tylenol #3 ordered for you." Karen responded.

"TC#3!" The patient looked around the group with a disgusted face. "TC#3! Candy, they do nothing, Doc."

Karen turned to Lee W. "He has gone through the morphine claiming it did nothing for him. He is obviously very streetwise."

"Yaw-all want to go home?" Lee W. asked of the man. Turning to the group. "What are yaw-all going to do for pain control?"

The man spoke up. "Blue Dynamite will work. Ya maybe one hundred of them." The man lay back, crossing his arms and fixating a smile on Karen.

Lee W. looked confused. Karen responded: "he's talking about Percocet, 15-30 the kind with no Tylenol in them."

"Can we look at you, Mr. McNulty." Lee W. closed the bedside curtain.

"Ya, Ya, sure." The man said as he kicked off the sheets and raised the nightgown, exposing himself, all the while smiling at Karen.

Lee W. took his dressing off as the man started wailing. "Be careful, dude, that's my johnson yaw-all got there." Once the dressing was off, they saw a well healing circumcision incision below the glans or head of the penis. At the base of the penis was a small plastic drain. A swollen penis was visible.

The group closed the bedside curtain, and they drifted off into the hallway. "Okay, the guy is a character. Thompson I want yaw-all, not Karen, to DC his drain. The guy can go home. Send him with a week of Keflex," said Lee W. referring to an antibiotic. He turned to the intern. "Does the pharmacy stock that Percocet prescription?"

"Ya I think so."

"Send him home with 25 of those and no refills. He'll probably sell them. Send him as well on a stool softener. That med is constipating. Thompson, you talk with the guy. Make it a life or death matter!" Now emphasizing he said. "He is not to tug or use his member for any purpose other than voiding for 30 days. Ha... fat chance that will happen. Reinforce that, however. He might never get an erection again, sort of thing. Or that the penis has been known to spontaneously fall off in even lesser cases, if used prematurely."

The ward rounds finished with the group discussing a few questions. Lee W. had the governor in the back of his mind, and the entourage made its way to the ICU.

In the ICU there was another banner across the wall above the ward clerk announcing UTMB as Texas' choice. While there was not a caricature of Lee W., Schlomo Goldine had hand signed the banner in six inch letters thanking the surgical team and staff. After the group's arrival, everyone spied out Lee W. and stopped their work to congratulate him.

A television above the ward clerk's desk blasted the breaking news. There was the man, Schlomo Goldine giving a press conference. It looked to be a repeat, taped the night of the Governor's surgery.

"Governor J.T. Splintter is resting in the UTMB surgical intensive care unit. They list him as stable. He has asked me to repeat our thank you to the surgical staff and especially Doctor Hickok for their timely and professional treatment. We know that a difficult vein of Leukowitz contributed to the length of his case."

The man badgered on as Lee W. turned a shade of gray. Thinking to himself, he lamented: "oh, the vein of Leukowitz?" It was a departmental joke, and now it was on nationwide television. He wondered if it might soon find its way to the Gray's Anatomy text book.

Thompson Smith started laughing. "Man yaw-all told them about that!" It really impressed the resident with his attending, patting him on the shoulder. He reached into his pocket and produced an orange and white lettered card with the new UTMB logo and Lee W.'s caricature. "Can I have your autograph, Lee W. Hickok, MD?"

Karen Green asked Thompson what the vein of Leukowitz was. She noted the definition in her scut filled notebook to look up later. The medical students were scrambling looking through their pocket sized Merck manuals thinking they had missed something from their recent anatomy classes.

Lee W. just shook his head. Downing several antacids from the nurse's cart, he moved to the nurse's station, grabbed the Governor's chart and began flipping through it. Moving now to the man's door, the others circled around him. A sign on the door indicated that all visitors must be approved by Schlomo Goldine. The nurse exiting the room was happy to see him. She indicated that the Schlomo man was in the room. She would ask if Lee W. could see the Governor.

The nurse disappeared into the Governor's room. In her absence, Lee W. tried to straighten out the med-students. "Forget about the vein of Leukowitz. Yaw-all won't find it in any textbook."

As he was trying to explain, the nurse appeared out of the door. "He will be out in a moment to talk to you, Doctor Hickok. In the meantime, between you and me, that man is mean. He now wants me to take off the Governor's sequential compression boots. He hasn't allowed us to get him moving yet. The man told the Governor he need not cough if it hurts. The Governor's still intubated because he won't breathe deeply. Schlomo supports him. Is there something you could do, Doctor Hickok?"

Lee W. just stared at the nurse. This case was taxing the man. He had a poor feeling about this Schlomo guy already. When he thought of the man's first name, the term *schlong* came to mind.

Soon Schlomo appeared. He was a short squat man, broad at the waist, with a complicated cantilevered comb-over. Dressed in a brown plaid three piece suit a pinch too short, with black shiny cowboy boots, the man was actually still wearing a surgical mask. By its appearance, Lee W. suspected it was the same one from surgery Friday night.

"Doctor Hickok, so nice to see you." Schlomo said with a high-pitched drawl. He greeted him with the same limp shake. "What can we do for you?"

"I would like to see the Governor. If it is okay with yaw-all."

Schlomo looked at the urology team with a scowl. "Not all of you I would hope?"

"That's okay professor, we all got lots to do," Thompson said looking to Karen Green and the two med-students. Together they decided that rounds were over.

Thompson looked at Lee W. who shook his head. "I will see yaw-all for afternoon rounds."

After the entourage broke up the man approached Lee W. "Did I give you one of my cards?" Schlomo asked him slowly, looking directly into his eyes. Lee W. remembered the business card laying exposed in the OR trash hamper. He put out his hand, and the man slipped the old water damaged card into his hand as he led the Doctor into the ICU room.

The Governor lay flat on his back, asleep, still on the ventilator. The nurse was at his bedside reluctantly slipping off the sequential compression boots which were plastic sleeves that encased the patient's legs, delivering alternating pressure to compress and prevent blood clots.

Lee W. turned to Schlomo who was watching the Governor. He forced himself to not look down at the short man's comb-over. "Mr. Goldine. Yaw-all shouldn't take the boots off, what with his risk of blood clots. You know that you are putting him at risk of throwing a clot?"

"Call me Schlomo Lee W." The man said with a toothy grin. "Well, the Governor has left me in charge. He tells me that the boots itch and the Governor has indicated that he wants them off. He wrote me a note concerning this." The man held up his gold embossed personalized clipboard with some scribbled notes on a yellow tablet. He explained how the nurses were torturing the man, demanding him to cough and deep breathe. They even wanted the man to sit in a chair. Schlomo reported that all of this was unacceptable to the Governor.

Lee W. listened, then instructed the man on the need to deep breath, cough, and move to prevent blood clots and pneumonias. He went on further. "Mr. Goldine er... Schlomo. Yaw-all should let the doctors take charge. They know what is best."

"Yes," was all that Schlomo said. He placed his hand on the Doctor's shoulder and ushered him to the door. Lee W. left the room with some concern, however. The future would show how right the Doctor was.

CHAPTER 5

Post Operative Day Number Four

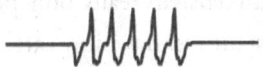

Abbott T. Frankenstein, MD, as with his namesake, was a huge hulk of a man. He stood introspectively at six foot five in well-polished wingtip shoes, a size 58 extra-long imported Italian tailored navy blue suit, his brow crowned by a well-trimmed flattop without wings. Through the floor to ceiling windows of his fifth-floor office, the University President cherished the view of his kingdom, the University of Texas Medical Branch campus. Before him stood the *new* John Sealy bed towers surrounding the *Old* John Sealy facility. Behind the complex was the Texas Department of Criminal Justice Prison Hospital towering over the original 1890 Victorian Medical School building known affectionately as 'ole Red.' To his right was the Shriner's Burn Institute and the Jeanie Sealy Hospital. To his left the newly constructed Moody Medical library opening for business just that week. With those facilities and the other hospitals and buildings on the campus, the UTMB complex of 933 licensed hospital beds represented state-of-the-art health care in America 1983.

UTMB's success through the years had been mixed. Established as the State Hospital and Medical School in 1890, at the time it was the largest medical complex west of the Mississippi. Galveston was in its heyday, being the major port and site of trade for the huge state of Texas. In 1914 a simple ship channel, cut from the Gulf Coast to Houston, eventually undermined and bypassed the small island cities' economy. This route of trade decimated Galveston, allowing the neighboring city of Houston to out-pace the Gulf Coast city. A similar fate befell UTMB. As the political and economic vagaries of the Houston-Galveston relation ebbed and flowed, so did the Medical Branch. With the rise of Houston, the Medical Branch had grown stale, not keeping up with the world of medicine. Doctor Frankenstein arrived in 1975, and in the eight years as Medical Branch President, a world renowned facility, with an internationally respected faculty and massive building projects began. Its conclusion was so successful and Abbott Frankenstein's lifetime accomplishment, but things had to change. He was ready to move on.

The Governor, J.T. Splintter, played the key to Frankenstein's advancement. The two knew each other since their undergraduate days at the University of Texas in Austin. Frankenstein went on to medical school in Galveston at the Medical Branch. Splintter went on to the UT Law School and a successful corporate law practice in Austin, Texas. Frankenstein really only practiced clinical medicine for two years, accepting the Assistant Dean position after a death and then advancing through the Texas politically controlled UTMB administration. He was the President of the University now for eight successful years, where intense oil based investment and a building program brought nationwide recognition to the Gulf of Mexico island community.

It surprised Frankenstein, as much as anyone, when his longtime friend announced his candidacy for the Republican nomination for Texas Governor. His victory over the experienced incumbent was a political miracle, created in no small way by an upcoming political consultant, Schlomo Goldine. This man was now attached to the Governor by the hip, and Frankenstein, as with most of his colleagues, hated the man. The man was ruthless in his furthering of the Governor's career. He was nasty and took down opponents with brutal force. Now there were rumors of a Splintter run for the White House. Frankenstein could see a political comet in the man and hoped to hitch his future dreams on the tail of his old friend. He would have to take Schlomo Goldine with the Governor, and Frankenstein did not like that fact at all.

Rumors that the Texas Senate seat would open with the retirement of the longtime Democratic incumbent, circulated. Frankenstein was not new to Texas politics. He had served as the state's surgeon general, a thankless job lasting two years. Holding his own post at the University as President was a political job that kept him in Austin more time than here in Galveston. He felt himself as qualified as anyone for the post of Senator, but wanted the Governor's endorsement and support. When rumors that the heavy drinking Governor suffered from a pancreatic pseudo-cyst, the right constellation of events seemed to be in the works.

Doctor Mark Fields was a brilliant researcher who had pioneered the field of pancreatic transplant. In the dog lab the man was a master, but his reputation in the bellies of human species was not so prestigious. When contacted however, the Governor jumped at an opportunity to get out of the news media of the capital, and choose UTMB to have his surgery in what they thought would be a media quiet setting on the idyllic Gulf Coast. Frankenstein covered himself with the memo directing the entire medical staff to be on call from the hospital that night. He rightfully thought if in fact trouble with surgery occurred, someone else would bailout Doctor Fields. It was brilliant and worked to a tee. But then Lee W. Hickok got involved, and the media focused on this vein of Leukowitz midnight salvation by the good Doctor, and soon there was a media circus surrounding the event.

Frankenstein had a bad feeling now about the Governor's case. There were nosey media everywhere, and the massive blood loss experienced that night predicted a long and perhaps complicated post-operative course. He figured however, that the worst was over, and the Governor would have a quiet and uneventful recovery at UTMB, his plans for political advancement still be in place. Something about that vision troubled the man.

Frankenstein sat down at his massive desk and began thumbing through the overwhelming paperwork produced by his position. The secretary buzzed the man, speaking quietly as not to antagonize the often irritated Frankenstein, when she announced a visitor who wished to speak to him. When he realized it was that Schlomo Goldine, his peptic ulcer, began acting up. Before ushering the man into his office, he swigged a bottle of Maalox from his desk drawer, careful to clean the chalky debris from his lips with his breast handkerchief. He then decided to not get up and meet the man at his office door, instead telling the secretary to bring the man in.

When the midget of a man appeared at his office door, Frankenstein rose reluctantly and accepted a limp handed handshake. Towering over the man gave Frankenstein a unique view of the cantilevered comb over the man was sporting. Concrete only could solve the engineering problem with his hair. Offering the man a seat on his settee, he buzzed his secretary to bring in a pot of Tea.

"What can I do for you, Mr. Goldine?"

In his high pitched whiney voice the man answered the President. "Call me Schlomo, Doctor Frankenstein. I have some concerns. As you know the Governor's surgery was successful and he is stable, recovering nicely in the intensive care unit of your fine institution."

"Yes, I was sure that his medical concerns are best handled here at UTMB."

Suzie the secretary knocked quietly and not waiting for an answer brought in a pot of Grandma Rae's Black Tea blend from the Panhandle of Texas in a Chinese porcelain serving tray and pot. She poured the President's brew and added sugar as he required, asking the visitor's desire.

After Suzie left the room, the conversation continued. "What complaints, or you said concerns, are you having Schlomo?"

"I have concerns about the care that is being given here to the good Governor. As you know during his incapacity I serve at the Governor's bequest. As his Chief of Staff, I am selected to make his medical decisions while he is incapacitated." Removing a notarized Advanced Care Directive document from his name embossed clipboard, the man laid it down with fanfare on the coffee table. "As you can see this Advanced Care Directive is legally drawn and signed giving me the position of deciding health care decisions."

A health care directive is a legal document used in near death situations where a family member can decide about end-of-life care for an incapacitated family member. In Frankenstein's experience it was not appropriate for this situation, as all possible medical care would be given without fail to this powerful man.

"We will do everything in our power. We do not need a document except to establish wishes when incapacitated near death. What is it you want to control?"

"As this directive indicates, I am to decide on all health care decisions."

This graven grab for power appalled Frankenstein. He had underestimated the man. Typically, an advanced directive dictated only the decision to resuscitate or not near the time of death. Here the man wanted to control day-to-day decisions on the Governor's medical care. Frankenstein said nothing, continuing to think.

"The staff is incompetent. They seem to not care about the Governor's comfort. My God, they have not even fed him yet. The Governor's stomach is very unpredictable and needs very fine adjustments to his diet. Your staff doesn't seem to understand that."

Frankenstein laughed to himself, careful not to let on to the man. "Well, he can't eat anything yet. He has had major abdominal surgery and the bowels are non-functional. This is called an ileus and will resolve by itself, but not for a week or so. During that time the bowel needs to be at rest, taking no food or fluids. He'll be fed as soon as his gut can tolerate it. In the meantime he is getting fed intravenously."

"Well, that does not explain the staff's insistence on coughing and moving. He is in agony. The staff does not seem to care!"

"Again there are reasons for this. After abdominal surgery, the patient must do things to clear his lungs. It is very important in preventing pneumonia. The staff is just carrying out the attending physician's very correct orders, Mr. Goldine... er, Schlomo."

"What about this directive?" Goldine held the document up in the air.

"Any order on the patient's care can only come from a physician number one, and number two a physician with hospital privileges, that is the hospital grants certain physicians the power of order writing. You cannot make day-to-day decisions. Your directive allows you to make end-of-life decisions, but it is up to a physician to direct the nurses in all care."

Schlomo stood in anger. "You could direct the staff to obey my instructions, Doctor Frankenstein. Certainly the orders for getting out of bed. That is too much he needs strict bedrest."

The discussion was getting out of control. This was a powerful man, and Frankenstein dearly wanted his cooperation. "Okay, Schlomo. Sit down and drink your tea."

"Look sir," Frankenstein said touching the man on his shoulder. "I will look over the situation and where I can try to carry out your wishes."

"We must practice state-of-the-art medicine, however. Unfortunately, it is uncomfortable after surgery. The Governor needs to first off have nothing orally until his bowel functions. Second, he must cough and deep breath and move. I can't overrule orders that are following established clinical guidelines." Frankenstein said now calmly, his huge hands pointing out the salient points.

So these two disagreed on their understanding of the health care directive, understanding each other's point of view, to some degree. Schlomo Goldine thought he won the argument, but would find the staff no more receptive to his input. Frankenstein hoped that he could mollify the situation and not alienate this powerful man. Neither one would have his way.

• • •

Lee W. Hickok parked on Mechanic Street adjacent to an old restored Victorian building belonging to the law firm of Farber and Calhoun. He glanced at the keyed door of his Datsun, hoping that the Superman logo would carry the day. He dressed for business, the day his educational half day where he would usually take care of loose ends. Dressed in a navy blue blazer, pink button-down collar shirt and blue and pink tie, his beige slacks were stretched over the usual pair of boots, today's being black lizard skin. He crossed the street in a hurry, ten minutes late as always, and entered the raised veranda surrounded building.

Andrew Calhoun saw him in a corner office as soon as the man arrived. He was a stick thin African-American man dressed in a black three piece suit, his appearance completed by the Cornrowed hairstyle.

"Lee W. how yaw-all doing?" The man said with a firm handshake. "I haven't heard from you for quite some time. How is that ex? Still beautiful but perplexing?" He wondered about the ex-wife Amber, the divorce that he had helped fashion.

Lee W. shook his head affirmatively. "Hi Andy. Yes, she is fine... beautiful... and stubborn."

"Still thinking of reconciliation? My services are always available there."

Lee W. looked down at his cowboy boots. Mindlessly, he reached for and popped a breath mint. "Well, I am working on that Andy, but I'm here concerning different circumstances."

"Oh?"

"DWI, last Friday night or actually Saturday morning. New Year's day, in fact."

The two moved to the attorney's desk. Calhoun reached to the floor and pulled out of his briefcase a morning edition of the Galveston County Daily News. "Have anything to do with this?" He said pointing to a picture of Lee W. The headline read, brilliant surgeon sure surgery successful. "What's this vein of Leukowitz thing, Lee W.?"

Lee W. put his hand over his face and sighed.

"Never mind, I wouldn't understand that anyway. But Lee W. the DWI was just after that surgery, wasn't it?"

Lee W. thought about his answer. Deciding to confide in his lawyer, what with attorney-client privileges, he described the situation. "Well, on my way home from that surgery I was stopped, and they found an open container in my car."

"What about the DWI?"

"Yes zero point one eight."

Calhoun began taking notes on a yellow legal-sized pad of paper. "Was that blood or breath-o-lyzer?"

"Breath."

"Were you drinking?" "Yes."

"How much and when Lee W."

Here Lee W. stretched the truth. "Just two drinks about two hours after surgery."

"You weren't drinking before the surgery?"

"No." Lee W. said emphatically, a lie.

"Why did the officer stop you?"

"Right taillight infraction."

"How did he find the open container, and what are we talking about a beer?"

"Whiskey bottle. I had it right on the passenger seat in my briefcase. The snout was visible."

"I don't remember any other run-in with the law on your record. Any prior's Lee W.?"

"Not even a traffic ticket in my driving life."

"Well, the officer had probable cause to stop you with the taillight infraction, though that is not something they usually stop proper citizens for. What were you driving?"

"My Datsun 240 Z," Lee W. said proudly.

"Well, that's why, a hot car. Me myself now I drive a rat- trap, 68 Honda Civic. Never troubled. I see some problems on the probable cause to search your car, however, that is find the whiskey bottle. In the state of Texas it is clear. Open containers of alcohol give probable cause for field sobriety tests and breath or blood alcohol levels. If you refuse the breath, they can forcibly draw blood. Zero point one eight is not equivocal as it is quite over the legal limit. My guess is you are looking at, with your record and standing in the community, a 3 month suspension of your license. You will be able to drive to work and other necessary activities. But that is about it. Now I can't guarantee that, depends in part on the Judge you get."

They did not know how true that last statement was at the time.

· · ·

Amber agreed to go to dinner with Lee W. After the episode at the police impound, her decision pleasantly surprised and encouraged the man. But then she loved Luigi's Ristorante Italiano on the historic Strand district in old Galveston. Lee W. stopped after clinic for a haircut at Bob and Bill's hair saloon on the seawall. Whether it was Bob or Bill was not obvious, the two being identical twins. La King's Confectionery on the Strand for his daughter's favorite peanut brittle was the next stop and was on his way to Patti's florist next to Gerland's grocery store on University Avenue. He parked his Superman tagged Z car in front of the graying yellow color Grocery store. It was an aging rundown store, the paint chipped, and needing maintenance for years. A grocery employee came out of the store to his left. The man was grinning as he held an enormous rat by the tail. "I found it on the bread aisle," he said, as if he expected Lee W. to find this amusing. Not waiting for his response, the man bashed the rodent with a shovel, turned and returned to the store. As he entered the florist next door to the store, he wondered how he had shopped at such a place during his time in medical school. Patti's was a small, fresh place; jam-packed with beautiful flowers and smelling of roses. He asked the store owner for a recommendation on what to get his ex something other than the dozen rose's he so typically gave to her. Patti suggested a bowl of flowers that Amber could plant and he agreed to an arrangement of fresh lilies, carnations, alstroemeria in pretty shades of pink, arranged in a wicker basket. The florist thought they were soft, feminine and full of beauty. Lee W. did not know a germanium from a daisy. He did not know what she would like, but he trusted the woman.

He made it to Amber's town house on Seventh Street and Seawall with fifteen minutes before their seven PM reservation at Luigi's. He was a chronically late arriver, but was so excited to see Amber. It was cold for the Gulf city at 48 degree's, and he left his car and heater running, making sure to turn on Amber's seat heater.

He was nervous as on a high school date as he stepped onto the front porch and knocked politely. Kellie answered the door. She had just come from the gym and dressed in pink spandex tights and a black sweet shirt. He told her how beautiful she looked and she did, her blonde hair short and curly, her amazing blue eyes so joyful. The peanut brittle was a hit, and Kellie yelled upstairs for her Mom, indicating her Dad's arrival. Kellie pulled out a breath mint from his front pocket and popped it into her mouth.

Her descent down the stairs dazzled the man as always. She dressed in a burgundy sleeveless pull over mini dress with matching heels, her curly blonde tresses done just so, a brown short waisted leather coat casually thrown over her shoulder. He told her she was a vision as he presented the flower arrangement, and when he told her she could plant them she just smiled a knowing smile.

"Your handsome as well, Lee W." she said as she fixed his charcoal tie and kissed him on the cheek. Hate was perhaps too strong of a word for their relationship, but after his fling with a medical student and what with his drinking, the woman had been disappointed repeatedly, and her free willed temper was often the only emotion that she would give to the man. She seemed anticipatory as he opened the passenger door of his Datsun for the beautiful woman. Lee W. was glad that the Superman keyed door on the driver's side was hidden in shadows, not wanting to refresh her recent memory of the man.

Luigi's was packed as usual, and they delayed their table for a few moments. Lee W. led the woman by her hand to the Victorian restored mahogany bar and got them drinks. His was a double bourbon on the rocks, her's a glass of white wine. Amber looked at the two drinks with a hidden air of disappointment. She took the wineglass reluctantly, forcing a smile. They secluded their table, lit only by candles. A violin playing maestro soon serenaded them.

"Can I get the signora a glass of wine?" The mustached, bow-tied and cummerbund wearing waiter asked.

"We'll have a bottle of Pedernales Cabernet Sauvignon. Do you have the 77 version?" Lee W. said, referring to his favorite Texas wine. When Amber looked at him with that look, he indicated that they were celebrating and that it would go well with any of her favorite dishes.

The waiter handed a menu to each and placed a basket full of bread on the table. He introduced himself as Giuseppe and lit two more candles. After bringing the wine, opening it and allowing a sip, Lee W. judged the bottle satisfactory.

"Would you like an appetizer?" The waiter wondered, and he suggested the Carpaccio, a dish of raw meats and fish. When served he enquired about their entrée's, Amber having the Lobster Ravioli and Lee W. veal Ossobuco.

"What are we celebrating?" Amber wondered, as she buttered a piece of Italian bread and nibbled.

"Reconciliation."

Amber smiled and then looked down at her lobster. Cooked in a light tomato vodka sauce replete with and sauteed in wine, it was her favorite. She loved it, but was afraid of what her ex-husband was talking about. "You have disappointed me so many times Lee W."

"Never again, Amber."

"You drink too much, you know, I can't go through that anymore."

The question stopped his request for a second bottle of wine. Lee W. quietly ate his veal.

Amber reached for her purse. She pulled a copy of the Galveston County Daily News. "Lee W." She said, trying to change the subject.

Lee W. shook his head and smiled. "Not that. You are a hero! What's the vein of Leukowitz? Don't ask Amber." After saying this, he worried about insulting her. Amber was a brilliant woman, a graduate of UT with a biology degree. "Do you really want to know?"

"Yes, I really want to know." She said, mimicking his tone of voice.

Lee W. looked up as the waiter refilled their water glasses. He then went on. "It's a joke. There isn't a vein of Leukowitz except around here. Ken Leukowitz, remember him? He was a resident two years or so before me. This vertebral vein that drains into the renal vein, he tore that many times to the point that Fadi named the vein after him." Lee W. referred to Dr. Fadi who was the chief of the urology department at the University. "How the paper got wind of this is incredible." He briefly described what went on in the operating room on New Year's Eve. He down played the hero aspect and told her the Governor is still in the ICU.

The waiter appeared again. They wanted to share a crème Brule, and Giuseppe soon returned with the dish. As they ate, Amber opened the paper to an inside page. "I know you don't like Dear Abbey, but she has a great survey on alcoholism." Looking the man in the eyes she said: "You know you're an alcoholic Lee W. I hate to break up this beautiful setting, but will you take this test she has if I read it to you?"

Lee W. left the last spoon full of the Brule for Amber. He smiled and told her he would.

"Okay, answer these questions Lee W." Amber pulled out her red rimmed reading glasses and began. "Do you drink alone?" Amber recalled in her head the so many times that Lee W. would drink sitting home, reading, or watching football.

Lee W. thought about the question. Who doesn't he thought? He remembered the so many times that he would drink in his office. "Not really," he said.

Amber looked at him over her glasses with a knowing look. She shook her head negatively. "Tell the truth, Lee W. Here's the second question. Do you ever go into a bar by yourself?" Amber reviewed the times she had looked for him and found him in a bar drinking by himself.

Lee W. thought of the Elephant's Ear bar right down the Strand from this restaurant where he drank till the wee hours at least once a week. He had not thought about the fact that he was generally alone. "Not anymore." The man said.

Amber let that slide and quickly asked another question. "Do you drink until you pass out occasionally?" She remembered the weekend he had gone missing. Only her diligence found him in his office, passed out under his desk. She was a small woman and how she got him to the car was a miracle.

Lee W. thought of finding himself on the Galveston beach, a brown paper bagged fifth of bourbon by his side. Lying again, he said: "Not for a long time."

The check came as the woman continued. "Do you ever lose time when drinking?" To this the woman could not attest, this being something only the drinker would know.

Lee W. recalled just the other night when he could not remember going to bed. His life was replete with examples of lost time. "I don't remember," he said, laughing now.

Lee W. could see Amber's temper being tested. With some flourish, she wadded up the paper and dropped it under the table. She looked long and hard at Lee W. with disappointment. Lee W. realized that Amber had made her point, but then who was Dear Abbey to label him?

After dinner the two walked with joined hands along the historical Strand district. It was a chilly night, but the air was clean and crisp. The street was lit up by historically correct appearing gas lamps, and the nightlife populated the quaint shops, restaurants, and bars. The night was a time to remember for Lee W. He kissed the woman after opening the door to his car, and Amber seemed to return the affection.

As they drove, Lee W. wondered about the chances of renewing their relationship.

"What happened to us, Amber?" In his mind he knew, his drinking so often conflicting with his marriage. They had a wonderful daughter, however, and a return to an affectionate relationship was so important.

"I love you, Lee W., but you are an alcoholic, and you love the bottle more than me."

She was partly right. He knew he was an alcoholic, and at the time stopping was not in his mind. He remembered one weekend of abstinence. He had the shakes by Sunday, and only the return to alcohol relieved them. He made it two days another time, a friend taking him to the Astros game. One beer and he was drinking again.

When they parked at the townhouse, he reminded the woman that he had their waterbed at his place. He remembered how wild she could be.

Amber smiled sadly. Behind this she seemed tempted. She seemed to think about it, bringing Lee W. in to stay at her place, but she did not want to confuse her daughter. "Kellie is home. She wouldn't understand. I need to fix her breakfast before school tomorrow."

And so the night ended, Lee W. encouraged. He was realistic at the same time. He drove down Seawall sure to obey each traffic law. He thought about that morning when Amber picked him up at the station. Tonight was a success, he realized, the woman had not once called him a horse's ass.

CHAPTER 6
Post Operative Day Number Five

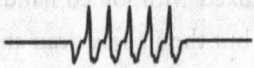

Sentimentally, this last patient of the day was a difficult one for Lee W. Entering the room he shook the frail hands of the 92-year-old man and his elderly wife. The patient suffered from castrate resistant metastatic prostate cancer. Here the prostate cancer was progressing even after the removal of the testicles. It is the lethal stage of a very common cancer. Lee W. exchanged pleasantries as he summed up the man in his mind. Mr. Harris lost weight since his last visit, obvious even without a scale. As usual, however, he dress was neat, in recently pressed slacks and long sleeve shirt, his attire completed with a veteran's ball cap. He had bruises on his arms and right side of his face. Luckily, he was voiding well.

They had been experimentally following a blood test called prostate specific antigen or PSA. It had much promise for the future as a marker for the disease. Mr. Harris' PSA was high and increasing each visit. This goes along with the clinical impression of progression. There are a few anti-cancer drugs used in this situation. They had tried all in the recent past, with side-effects and lack of improvement dictating stoppage. Lee W. was sad as he realized he had only his friendship left to offer the couple.

Mr. Harris, as always, was sincerely interested in Lee W's family. They had never met, but he remembered seeing the picture of his daughter, Kellie, over the years. The patient was a wonderful man who loved his urologist. The wife had brought in the Galveston paper and asked for an autograph. It embarrassed Lee W, but hid his discomfort. He eventually signed the front page for the stooped old woman, a photograph of him looking like a smiling fool.

They talked again about death. Lee W. reminded the couple that he was a Methodist. He believed in God and the afterlife. Harris' were Baptists and believed the same. They wondered, as usual, whether the good Doctor was attending Church, the man so sick but still concerned for him. They ended their visit with a promise to return to the clinic in one month. Lee W. believed this visit today would be Mr. Harris' last. He found himself sad; the couple becoming dear friends. He helped both walker using people out of the room and on their way. Lee W. hoped that he would see them again.

.　.　.

The Chief of Urology, Doctor Fuad Fadi, wanted to see Lee W. after his last patient. They announced the informal appointment that morning with a handwritten sticky note attached to his door. Lee W. returned to his office, locking the door. Silently he removed his tumbler and bourbon and downed a double shot. Breath mints completed the routine. He walked around the clinic to the larger office directly opposite his own. Lee W. knocked, then ushered in by Fadi.

"Lee W. come in and have a seat. How is your daughter?"

"She's fine Fuad." Lee W. sat in a leather chair arranged at the foot of the man's cherry wood desk. Taped to his bookcase was another annoying poster announcing Texas' Choice with the Lee W. cartoon. The urologist looked at the poster with embarrassment.

Fadi seemed to smile at Lee W.'s reaction. Charts clutter the man's desk. He was smoking a large cigar which was burning in an UTMB glass ash tray. Doctor Fadi was a distinguished Middle Eastern man with a bushy black mustache and graying hair. He dressed that afternoon in a button down white collared shirt with a yellow silk tie, and khaki brown pants. His navy blue jacket hung neatly on a brass and cherry wood coat rack in the corner of his office. He was Lebanese, with an outstanding resume. It comprised time in the 70's as chief of surgery at the American University in Beirut. While a skilled surgeon and physician, the politics of being chief were not his forte. He once told Lee W. that he hated being chief, but Frankenstein strongly encouraged him to continue.

"What can I do for you today, Fuad?" Lee W. asked starting the conversation after small talk.

Fadi seemed reticent and began talking about department events. "We will lease a lithotripter." He said with just a hint of a Lebanese accent. Here the man referred to an extracorporeal shock wave lithotripter, a shock wave machine used to treat kidney stones. There had been rumors of this for months. This machine, which would come to be used by urologists across the country, would eventually change the nature of kidney stone treatment in the United States over the next decade.

Lee W. was very excited about this. He had taken several classes about the new technology. While he knew that there was something deeper as the source of the meeting, he allowed the man sometime to discuss such an important acquisition. "When does it arrive?"

"Next month. It will be out back in a trailer each Wednesday. I want you to spearhead the use of this machine by our department. At first all lithotripter cases will go to you. Then eventually other members of the department will become certified and do their own cases."

Lee W. laughed quietly to himself, knowing a secret about the machine. "Using that machine is so easy Fuad. I am stealing your money by doing all the cases."

The machine was nearly failsafe. The patient's kidney stone was located on an x-ray table, and the machine focused shock waves at just the right rate and direction automatically. The cases were done with anesthesia, so the patient had no pain. After the procedure, the great majority of patients could go home with oral pain medicine. During the 80's and 90's, the machine would revolutionize the treatment of the common stone in the United States. Lee W. and UTMB would be at the forefront of using this modern technology.

There was an uncomfortable silence in the room. Again something other than a lithotripter was on the chief's mind. He turned to the bookcase and removed the poster. "Texas's Choice- UTMB. Quite a resemblance to you, do you not think Lee W.?" Fadi pointed to the caricature and laughed. "What went on that night?"

Lee W. described the case for perhaps the hundredth time. When he reached the point of the bleeding vertebral vein, he did not call it the vein of Leukowitz. Fadi had coined the term. He was such a polite man, however, that he did not approve of its use, as it disparaged Joe Leukowitz.

"Lee W. there is something else that I wanted to talk to you about."

Here it comes, thought Lee W.

Fadi stood and moved to his file cabinet in the room's corner. Using keys from his pants' pocket, he opened the bottom drawer and removed a manila file folder labeled with Lee W's name. He returned to his desk with the file. Opening the folder, he read silently a short memo by himself. He looked up into Lee W.'s eyes. "I'll get right to the point. You were stopped and arrested for driving while intoxicated after the Governor's case?" Lee W. sat quietly, diverting his eyes to the floor. The statement was surprising. How would the man know such a thing? He looked up at Fadi and cleared his throat, nodding his head affirmatively.

"You are quite the hero around here. It's lucky because Frankenstein is aware of your arrest and has said very little about this."

It now became obvious how the information became available.

"Lee W. were you drinking before the surgery that night?" Commonly known throughout the hospital, Lee W. drank. His breath mints could not hide the smell of distilled Kentucky bourbon. It was a joke, however; the man could operate and take care of patients so that no one had ever cared. Lee W. had always believed that other physicians drank as well, but he had no concrete evidence to support that.

Lee W. considered his options. He decided to lie. "Of course not Fuad, I was on call!"

Fadi weighed Lee W.'s answer. He seemed relieved by the response. Even though he suspected a lie, he accepted the reply. "Good, my man." Fadi picked up his cigar and lit it with a silver engraved lighter. He offered one to Lee W.

"Thank you. For after dinner." Lee W. took a cigar, placing it in his shirt pocket.

There was an uncomfortable silence as the two sat looking at one another. Fadi stood and accompanied Lee W. to the door. He mentioned more about his plans for the lithotripter. Lee W. then told him of the penile fracture case. They completed their discussion by laughing.

Once in his office, Lee W. was distraught. He had just lied to a dear friend. He poured himself some bourbon and downed it with a gulp. He reviewed the events of the last week as the alcohol calmed him. Concern that the hospital administration knew of his arrest overcame him. No one seemed to care however, and for that he was thankful. DWI's are common, the hard drinking man decided. His lawyer had outlined what would happen. Three months without a license and the ability to drive to and from work; it seemed like an easy sentence. He would never drive with an open container again. He convinced himself that absent the bourbon bottle that night, Willie Washington would have let him go. Lee W. held his alcohol; the officer would never have suspected drinking if he had been smart about concealing the bottle. He was convinced that he passed the field sobriety tests with flying colors. A breath-a-lyzer level of 0.18 was borderline, he incorrectly rationalized. He thought about his drinking. Amber's quiz entered his mind. Guilt engulfed him.

The clinic was dark and empty when Lee W. left for the night. He walked past the entrance, the enormous poster still clinging to the wall, his caricature staring down upon the man with accusation. Lee W. stopped and looked up at the ridiculous piece of propaganda. He placed his briefcase on the floor, jumped and grabbed the bottom of the poster, tearing it down with deliberation. It was in the trash can and he was out of the clinic within minutes now, feeling a sense of satisfaction.

Lee W. was finding the restoration of a turn of the century Victorian home quite a project. The home at one time had been the Galveston mayor's. It had a storied history having made it through the 1900 hurricane, considered the worst natural disaster in the country's history. It was located on the secluded 63rd Street, near but well off of the busy thoroughfare, Seawall. The home had a detached single space garage, a wraparound veranda porch, and was full of ornate woodwork. Lee W. had mortgaged the property for what it was worth but had little cash to pay for the labor. He had put himself through college working construction and considered himself proficient with the hammer and paintbrush. The restoration then was his, but it had lingered on for so long now that the man was tiring of the project.

When the door rang, Lee W. was in his Levi's and paint stained T-shirt. He had an ice cold Lone Star beer and was painting the walls of the great room. She appeared at the door without notice. Amber was holding the arrangement of flowers that Lee W. had given to her the night of their "date." She was a vision as always, her curly blonde hair pulled back with a pink and white headscarf. She too wore an old shirt, this one of Lee W.'s worn collared shirts with the sleeves rolled up. Levi's covered her too curvy to be fair lower frame. Pink tennis shoes completed the outfit to which Lee W. could only whisper "wow."

"Amber." The man said so surprised and excited. Amber planted a pleasant kiss on his cheek. "You can plant those flowers you know." Lee W. said repeating himself from the other night stupidly not knowing what else to say.

"I know, silly." Amber rubbed a small wad of paint off of Lee W.'s face. "That's what I am here for. I can't plant these at the townhouse. We don't even have a garden Lee W. Why don't we start one here?" The woman said excitedly.

Lee W. stepped out on the veranda. He took the arrangement from the woman after planting a responding kiss on her perfect cheek. "You look ready to work."

"I am. Where is a shovel?"

So they took time to dig a shallow hole and planted the arrangement just in front of the front porch. A good soaking from the garden hose finished the project.

Both washed their hands right there and entered the house after wiping their muddy shoes on the doormat.

"Oh, Lee W. you have finished so much since I have been over here." Amber said looking around the entry and great room. She really was opening a can of worms since the man could not remember her last visit. Both laughed uncomfortably.

Lee W. went down the stairs quickly to the basement. Here he had his "beer" fridge. Grabbing two Lone Star's he was back up to Amber before she knew he was gone. Both took a swig on their long necks, Amber setting her's aside while Lee W. finishing his quickly.

Lee W. guided Amber around the home, showing her some work he had done, but mainly discussing his plans. Boxes and boxes of tile, wooden flooring, and power tools lay scattered about. They went upstairs, the master bedroom painted and finished. The waterbed they had shared for some many years was old, but Lee W. could not comprehend acquiring a new one. Their clothes came quickly off, lying in a pile on the floor. The bed was in use the old-fashioned way, waves of water rolling and functioning as well or perhaps better than in past times.

When they had finished the two embraced in blissful harmony. Lee W. caressed Amber, softly rubbing her pale skin and beautiful curly blonde hair. It had been so long since the two had shared a bed or anything worthwhile. Their time together afterward was so relaxed and precious. It was short lived for the usual reason.

Lee W. reached to the nightstand and finished his Lone Star Beer, the thought of another tempting him. He rolled out of the waterbed and pulled on his boxer shorts. He was quickly off, returning with two cold beers.

Amber was dressing in haste when he returned. Lee W. was standing in the doorway, aware that he had made a mistake. She looked at the man and shook her head. Disillusioned, she continued dressing, anger now in the air.

Lee W. stood in his boxer shorts silently looking at the woman sadly. He lifted the two beers by their necks and set them aside quietly on the nightstand.

"You will never quit, will you Lee W.?"

Lee W. moved to the waterbed, throwing back the ruffled up sheets. "Amber, please get back in bed with me! I won't drink these." He said with sincerity. He moved to Amber's side, trying to gently coax her to lay down with him.

Amber thwarted his advance, angrily pushing him away and finishing dressing. When complete, she stood in the doorway and stared at Lee W. Disappointment was all over her face. "Nothing will happen good between us until you dry out, Lee W. I mean it! Your drinking reminds me of so many bad times. We may play around on dates and roll around on your waterbed, but you are a drunk and until you quit, you are just a horse's ass." She turned and left, her pink tennis shoes echoing down the stairs, the front door closing with a slam.

• • •

"The Governor needs some food. You are starving the man?" Schlomo Goldine came stomping out of the Governor's ICU room looking for someone to abuse. He was concerned for the Governor. He was the Governor's chief of staff, and nothing was more important to the man. After standing over the Governor he had seen the sadness in his face, the man unable to speak because of his endotracheal tube. He was not about to shirk his responsibility. He was the Governor's man and, as the hospital directive indicated, would stand up for him in his absence. He remembered illnesses of his own where chicken soup was used to remedy everything from chickenpox to the flu, and could not understand this hospital's negligence. He moved to the nursing station, looking for his closest victim.

Because of staffing shortages, Ms. Bonnie was the ward clerk on the ICU that day. Schlomo was huffing and puffing, stomping his small little cowboy boots, looking for his victim. Ms. Bonnie just stared at the man, shaking her head, sitting in control at the nurse's station. She had worked at the University longer than anyone could remember. No one could intimidate the woman. She was not a woman to be trifled with, something the man was not aware of.

Schlomo stared back at the woman, expecting an answer. When she did not answer, he said: "look here woman! What about the Governor?"

Ms. Bonnie grabbed the hospital chart and flipped quickly through the pages. "Here yaw-all." She said pointing to the diet instruction with a long flashy painted nail, holding the chart open for the man. They marked the diet as NPO, nothing per oral, and she told the man of the fact. "The Governor's NPO!" She said, returning the chart to the rack with a flourish.

"NPO, what is NPO?" The man asked in a just too loud fashion. A small crowd was gathering as the two faced each other down.

"That means he gets nothing, honey!" The ward clerk said with authority.

"That is my point entirely. The Governor has not eaten in three days. Some soup! Some water for heaven's sake! This hospital is killing the man!"

"He's NPO." Several in the crowd whispered as if it was a Godly order.

"Do you think I care about what your chart says? NOP or whatever; I want him fed! Here give me that chart!" The man yelled and stomped his boots. He grabbed the chart from the rack, removed his fountain pen, and started writing in the doctor's orders. *Feed the Governor* in bold black letters were written. Then he literally threw the chart back in the rack.

Schlomo turned to the crowd, and as if a cheerleader, prompted the group.

The violation of hospital protocol revolted Miss Bonnie. She stood now, the thin wiry woman towering over the tiny chief of staff. "I am warning you, Mr. Schlomo Goldine. Yaw-all can't write in the chart!" The man had committed a cardinal sin, from the ward clerk's perspective. Hospital policy was very clear, no one other than physicians granted hospital privileges could write an order in a patient's chart. Schlomo was not a physician and certainly did not have hospital privileges. They would recognize nothing the man could write in the chart, court directive or not. The ward clerk would make certain of this.

Ms. Bonnie picked up a red Jell-O bowl from an unused patient tray. She moved to the angry man and turned the bowl over on top of his carefully coiffured head. Without a word she moved to the phone. "Let me talk to Malcolm... Malcolm, this is Ms. Bonnie up here to the ICU. We have us a situation," she said, speaking to security. "We have us an unruly guest."

The Jell-O had an unexpected calming effect on Schlomo. Even the pompous man somehow knew that he had overstepped his authority. He took the Jell-O off of his head, grabbed a towel and disheveled his comb-over. Silenced for the moment, he paraded back to the Governor's room leaving the crowd behind.

Katy the nurse was busy inside of the Governor's room. She turned as Schlomo entered the room examining the red-tinged hairline.

"What happened to you Mr. Goldine?"

Schlomo dismissed the question. "The Governor needs something to eat young lady. How can you be party to this negligence!"

"Mr. Goldine, he is post-op. He is NPO and needs to be until he starts moving his bowel functions. If you feed him now, it will make him sick. He can suck on ice, though. It will just come back up his NG tube."

Schlomo repositioned his hair. Thinking for a moment it dawned on the man. "He can have ice?" The man wondered, calming down.

"As much as he wants, it will just come back up the NG tube."

"Honey, maybe that will make him happy."

Katy exited the room to get some ice chips. Schlomo looked at the Governor, trying to determine his wishes. The man silently looked up at his Chief of Staff, intubated with an endotracheal tube in his mouth. He looked at Schlomo with a frightful expression. He lifted his left leg and set it down with a jolt.

"Those boots, I know Governor." Schlomo said as he began struggling to take the sequential compression boots off. Once off, he stuffed them into the corner of the room's closet. Katy returned with ice chips. Malcolm, the head of hospital security, accompanied her. "Yaw-all will have to follow me," the big man said. There was not any arguing.

50

CHAPTER 7
Post Operative Day Number Six

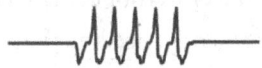

"Yaw-all doing so well, Governor!" The ICU nurse, Katy said comfortingly, standing at the patient's side. The young female aide stood at the foot of the bed, both women determined to get the man moving, this fine Wednesday morning.

Governor J. T. Splintter's thinning palate stood disheveled and greasy, his exposed chest showing more hair than his head. Sitting in the hospital bed, the man's rotund abdomen hung over the bedsheets. Covered with a white gauze paper taped dressing, bloody pancreatic drainage filled two grenade shaped bottles lying at his side. With great discomfort he grimaced, swallowing painfully secondary to the NG tube in his nostril. Repositioning the oxygen mask, the man cleared his throat, sucking on the glycerin swab, as Katy raised the head of the bed.

"We will get yaw-all up in a chair today." Katy said so one would think the man was going to the moon. The Governor shook his head. He opened his mouth and pushed out a swollen red tongue. Pointing to his wound with an IV containing hand, he spit out the words. "Pain... you bitch! Moving hurts like hell! Put my head back down."

"Governor!" The aide said with a startled look, as she moved to help the nurse.

The language did not surprise Katy, however, having had plenty of abuse thrown her way by her precious patient since his stealth like midnight admission Friday night. She wished Gladys, the head nurse, had not given this honor to her. Taking care of this *special* patient was more than the usual nurse's torment. More so, she really wished she did not have to get the man moving, what with the incision plaguing his every movement. However, orders were orders, and Doctor Fields AM note had said: *up out of bed to chair this morning without fail.*

The nurse disconnected the NG tube suction and lowered the bed rail. The two women began pulling the man's legs to the side of the bed.

"Get me a pain shot woman!"

"You just had 10 mg of morphine... ah Sir."

"I don't give a shit! What is your name?" The Governor said with a superior scowl, scrunching up his nearsighted eyes.

"Like I told you Katy, Sir."

"Where is S.G.? Schlomo, the man is worthless," said the Governor.

"What is a Schlomo?" The aide said as the two wrestled with the chief executive officer of the state of Texas.

Once in his bedside chair the Governor demanded some ice chips.

The aid disappeared conveniently, needing to help the nurse next door. Katy re-plugged the NG tube and turned to the hallway for the ice. As she returned, the Cardio-monitor was howling an ominous wail.

In the room she found an unresponsive Governor who had slid down in the bedside chair, hanging now from his NG tube. His eyes were closed, mouth open, tongue pushed out, his extremities sprawled in all directions as if he had fought. The Governor of Texas had a cardiac arrest.

Katy picked up the bedside phone and yelled for a code to be called. Code Blue calls loudly echoed throughout the hospital. The nurse cut the NG tubing with her scissors, and listened for breathing, which was absent. She jumped to his side and began cardio-pulmonary resuscitation (CPR).

Soon chaos filled the room with the usual cast of characters; internists, surgeons, nurses, respiratory technician, etc... each responding to the overhead announcement. There was bedlam and loud yelling as the room filled up. They moved the man to his bed, placed on a wooden backboard and put in trendelenburg position, legs up, head dangling. A youthful faced resident began crushing chest compressions to the spoken rhythm: "one and two and three and four and five, breath; one and two," ... and so forth. Anesthesia took over managing the airway with an ambu bag, pumping breath after breath between cycles of chest compressions. The medical officer of the day (MOD) stood as the captain of a fighting force at the foot of the bed. She was a senior internal medicine resident in charge of running the code; directing treatment, matters of ventilation, chest percussions, when to begin CPR, and most important, when to end it.

The room filled, talking and yelling bubbling over like shots at a busy rifle range. They passed medicines and infused them through IV's. Cardiac monitors ran off paper tracings. Large lights illuminated the scene.

"Who is this patient?" The MOD yelled. The ward clerk arrived, bringing the hospital chart.

A surgical resident spoke up, having been in on the midnight stealth surgery. "He's the Governor. J.T. Splintter! The man is a sixty-four-year-old male status post distal pancreatectomy for a pancreatic pseudo-cyst. The Governor is in post-op day number 6." The man grabbed the chart, thumbing through the admission history and physical as chaos weaves around him. Splintter is healthy with no cardio-pulmonary risk factors."

Schlomo Goldine entered the hectic room in a frightened pace. He stood at the foot of the bed aghast at the scene, silent. He looked to his embossed clipboard and his copy of the directive. Soon he was pale and sweaty, and as the crowd swarmed around him he fell down flat on his face. Two medical students drug the weighty man into the corner of the room and accessed him.

The CPR on the Governor with compressions and counting dominated the room. The man's eyelids were closed, his groin covered with a sheet, bounced to a ghostly rhythm. They drew syringes of blood, aides running errands to the central lab. The clerk returned paper results from screaming fax machines, physicians reading and relating their results.

· · ·

Frustrated, Mrs. Allen heard the overhead call for code blue. She had taken a momentary break, cramming her large body into the hallway water closet, now stuck unable to get out of the door. She turned and pulled the rope on the red safety switch and a small buzz and flashing lights begin over the door.

· · ·

The MOD stopped CPR. There is an expectant silence as they check pulses. There is no pulse and they restart CPR, the pace picking up. She orders one hundred milliequivalents sodium bicarbonate. Katy has pulled her med cart into the room. Pharmacy moves in and begins logging medical orders and supplying the drugs. A confusing scene, orders missed and forgotten.

"Stop CPR..., V-fib," the MOD yells. A rapid, irregular tracing runs off on a roll from the cardiac monitor. "Clear," she yells. The sound, "Crack," echoes through the room, as 300 joules of cardio-version current are conducted through the Governor's chest. The man jumps violently as if flogged by a glass tipped whip. There is no response and the cardiac resuscitation continues.

Without interrupting the process, anesthesia intubates the Governor. They force his head back in extension, and examine his vocal cords with a laryngoscope. They slip a tube down through his mouth and into his trachea. Bagging the tube begins, ventilating the lungs in the set rhythm.

There has never been a pulse. Except for the moment of irregular tracing on the monitor, the heart activity has been flat line. They stop CPR multiple times always with the same facts. There is no cardiac activity. They ask Anesthia to deliver a trans-cardiac dose of epinephrine. The man takes a large needle and syringe full of drug. He locates the correct landmarks on the chest and stabs the needle through the chest wall to deliver a dose of the drug. A pacemaker is used across the chest wall. With each stop of CPR, they find the same dilemma: there is no pulse. Lidocaine, epinephrine, amiodiorone, magnesium, calcium-chloride and tens of drugs are all delivered to the patient without success.

Doctor Fields arrives in the room. The man moves to the bedside scowling. Fields looks at Schlomo in the corner who has just received smelling salts. He steps to the side of the MOD. After accessing the situation he directs to the room. "Get me a chest tray." As the attending physician he officially takes over the CPR, but allows the MOD to direct the medical resuscitation.

• • •

Mrs. Allen made it out of the restroom. Using her weight, she broke through the door into the hallway. Another aide is running down the hall and passes her. The overweight woman runs alongside.

"Where's yaw-all going Becky?" Breathing heavily, Mrs. Allen wondered.

"They want a chest tray so I'm going to the OR." The two run to the OR, crossing the hospital and climbing two flights of stairs. They return with their precious possession, bursting into the Governor's room with pride.

• • •

The chest tray makes its way onto a bedside table. A gloved nurse opens the huge tray, revealing a slew of shiny instruments. Schlomo received help to his feet by members of the crowded room. He has on a lime green suit and they pull the jacket up and nearly off. His white starched shirt is pulled halfway out at the waist, revealing a small segment of grotesque belly. His comb-over is dead, the hair sticking straight up in the air. The man said nothing as he began to cry. The medical students ushered him out of the room.

Fields turns in disgust, returning to the bedside. Throwing his white jacket onto the floor, the crowd separates allowing him access.

"Stop CPR!" He stops the chest compressions and people move away from the bed. He empties an entire bottle of Betadine surgical soap on the chest of the man and removes the abdominal dressing. Someone tosses a pair of sterile gloves, which he puts on quickly.

"Scalpel," Fields yells as the OR nurse hands him a shiny blade. With one swipe he has a left thoracotomy incision. Blood spills down the chest wall and onto the bed. Within twenty seconds he has his gloved hand on the Governor's heart.

For twenty-five minutes the surgeon compresses the heart. Anesthesia continues bagging and ventilating him. Drugs are slipped into IV's silently. The mob continues on. Intermittently the surgeon stops massaging, accessing for spontaneous cardiac activity. There is none.

The MOD is the first to come to the surgeon's side. Slowly activity dies down. There is a silent buzz in the room. "He's gone," she whispers.

Fields watches the woman in silence, continuing massage for another minute. He stops one last time; the heart is not beating. He steps away from the bedside, removes his gloves and flips them onto the ground. The room clears, the noise and sad excitement dying down. Fields sits down in the bedside chair and stares across the room breathing deeply. Someone hands the man the hospital chart, and he begins a death note.

· · ·

It was Lee W. Hickok's operating day that morning. He was in and out of OR room four, supervising the residents. He passed the front desk as he saw Mrs. Allen, who was all excited.

"What is going on Mrs. Allen?" Lee W. asked the nurse's aide.

"Oh, Doctor Hickok, yaw-all should see what's going on with the Governor."

"What's going on Mrs. Allen?" Lee W. asked now having that bad premonitory feeling. She explains his cardiac arrest. The phrase *successful surgery* crosses his mind silently.

Lee W. moves to the ICU. People are pouring out as he enters the Governor's room. The floor is awash with med ampoules, paper drapes, gloves, reams of cardiac tracing tape, and discarded IV bags. The man was dead on the hospital bed with the head depressed in trendelenburg position. Except for a towel over his groin, he was naked. A bloody incision in his left chest lays open by a gleaming rib spreading retractor. His body is growing cold and blue.

At his bedside is Mark Fields, his white coat in a heap at his cowboy booted feet, only one of which covered with a blue disposable cover. Writing in the chart, he looked up at his colleague.

"What happened, Mark?" Lee W. asked quietly.

"Probably had a massive PE."

Here the Doctor referred to the probability that a blood clot or pulmonary embolism had killed the man. Fields returned to his chart work.

Lee W. stood at the bedside in silence. He pulled up the sheet to look at the man's leg. "Why no sequential compression boots Mark?" He wondered seeing the lack of boots to prevent blood clots.

Fields stands and looks at the Governor's naked legs. "Schlomo fucking Goldine." Fields said as he stood and walked out of the room.

CHAPTER 8
Newscast

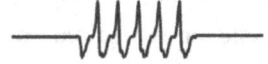

Abbott T. Frankenstein, MD stood silently, his huge stature overshadowing the small podium, while the mass of media crowded around. There was an ominous look on his face as he waited for the room to the quiet down. The chamber was buzzing, awash with anticipation. Something was up, gossip was flying, and the reporters smelled a big story. Somehow the press had sources inside the hospital. Rumors of the Governor's death were spreading.

Hospital staff gathered behind the University President. The attending physician, Doctor Mark Fields, stood eyes down-turned, a grimness covering his face. His shoulders showed, an exhausted countenance to the man. He had *cracked* the Governor's chest in front of the CPR crowd and conducted a hopeless, but skillful, open heart massage. Blood stains demonstrated his effort and remained, highlighting his white coat. Other administrators and physicians, and Doctor Lee W. Hickok grabbed at the last minute because of his popularity with the media, stood at attention.

Frankenstein raised one huge hand. He tapped on the microphone slowly and silenced the room. He then read from prepared remarks. "This morning the Honorable Governor of the great state of Texas, J. T. Splintter, expired at the University of Texas Medical Branch. He was just six days after extensive abdominal surgery for a nonmalignant pancreatic condition."

There was some murmuring from the rear of the auditorium. Frankenstein raised his gaze, paused sternly, and looked across the room as if a huge teacher silencing his class. The room quieted. He continued, his eyes glued to the prepared transcript. "After sustaining a large cardiopulmonary event, an extensive team of health care providers, including his attending physician, performed resuscitative maneuvers for over one hour. These attempts included cardio-pulmonary resuscitation, open cardiac massage, and electric shock and pacing. Though heroic, these maneuvers were unsuccessful at reviving his Honor. Governor Splintter was pronounced dead at 0830 January 6th 1983 by Doctor Mark Fields. I have informed his family and the Attorney General of the state of his demise."

There was a moment of silence in the crowd as it confirmed the event. Quickly, however, they recovered and regained their true aggressive nature, peppering the University President with chaotic questions. Like vultures, they fought for supremacy, pushing to the front of the room.

"What did the Governor die from?"

Once the University President recognized the question, moderate quiet enveloped the room. "Pending an autopsy, the exact answer is unknown. As I indicated it appeared that the Governor had a massive lethal cardio-pulmonary event."

"Is an autopsy going to be performed?"

"I think I answered that."

"Who presided over the resuscitation?"

"One of our best internal medicine residents, Doctor Karen Massey, was the medical officer of the day. She was in charge of the resuscitation. Doctor Fields was the attending physician."

"What happened to Schlomo Goldine?"

"Mr. Goldine is under Doctor's supervision, and I will not comment on his medical condition."

"Was this cardiac event predictable?"

"It was an unpredictable and unpreventable event not anticipated by the staff."

"Is it true that the Governor had dismissed his hospital staff?"

A curious, impatient expression crossed the face of the President. "That is absolutely not true!" There was a brief delay as Frankenstein stared down the media. The same individual made the enquiry that nailed the probable cause of the Governor's death. "Did the Governor have a pair of sequential compression boots on at the time of his death?"

Frankenstein took a deep breath. Almost involuntarily, he glanced over his shoulder at the medical staff. "I will not comment on any specific details of the Governor's care which would violate the physician-patient privilege."

"But he is dead!"

Frankenstein fumed, shaking his head negatively. "Again, I will not comment on any specific aspects of his care. And with that, I will end this press conference." Frankenstein left the podium quickly and disappeared into the hospital's bowels.

There was a frantic murmur in the room. They flung questions at the remaining members of the hospital staff. No answers were forthcoming. The rest of the team then disbursed as well.

.　　.　　.

Schlomo Goldine was not happy. He was so sure that he had a heart attack, the events in the ICU that morning just a blur. Doctor Karen Massey and several other internal medicine house staff stood at the foot of his bed telling the man that he was okay and could be discharged. At the heart of his disappointment, however, was the loss of his meal ticket. The Governor was his man. He had overseen a comet like rise to the Governor's mansion. His positions on the issues had vaulted the man to the premier Texas political position. Dreams of future White House bids were now history. And then there was Schlomo's condition. Witnessing a cardiopulmonary resuscitation in person is a brutal event. The things such as these would haunt him, at least Schlomo thought so.

Doctor Massey smiled at the man. "We have good news. Your electrocardiogram, your cardiac enzymes, and all blood tests are normal Mr. Goldine. It is very common to faint at the sight of things like you witnessed this morning. You'll do so much better out of the hospital."

Schlomo just looked up at the young physician with disdain. In his mind he was planning events that would ruin her medical career. They could have pity on the man and at least keep him in the hospital to hide him from the media. As he realized that he would have to leave, he planned his escape. He would take the Governor's limousine to the Hobby Airport in Houston. From there, a private plane would take the man back to Austin. Schlomo dismissed the group with a condescending wave of his hand.

When alone, Schlomo reached for the bedside phone. He dialed his office in Austin and lambasted his secretary just for old times. She was to arrange his immediate travel arrangements, including a limousine trip from what he called *this moldy hospital* to Hobby. He looked in the mirror attached to his bedside tray. What he saw of his comb over frightened the man, trestled hair standing up revealing a bald head. He showered, spent some time on his hair-do, changed into his favorite lime green suit, and was out of the room quickly.

The nurse's aide had a wheelchair for Schlomo's trip to the front of the hospital. Hospital policy required that discharged patients must be pushed in a wheelchair.

"Are you an idiot woman!" He said, dismissing the chair. "There is nothing wrong with me that won't be fixed by getting out of this place."

• • •

The young reporter who asked about sequential compression boots stood quietly at Lee W.'s office door, waiting for the man. Her name was Jennifer Harry, a tall and thin, young African- American woman. Neatly appointed in a trimmed Afro hair-do, she carried a leopard skin backpack thrown over her shoulder. She worked for the Houston network KTRK as a news reporter, a young newswoman just out of Rice University School of journalism in Houston. She interviewed the Doctor once before about a soft subject, the restoration of Galveston historical homes. The clinic staff therefore knew the woman, and they allowed her to wait for Lee W.

Lee W. was in a hurry. He shook the woman's hand, accepted her business card, and politely asked the reporter into his office. He was suspicious of her, what with the Governor's death. He remembered, however, his prior experience with the woman and the article she had penned about his house, and decided to trust her. "What can I do for yaw-all." Lee W. asked, opening up the office door and inviting her to sit next to his desk. A fresh cup of coffee was in Lee W.'s hand. He thought of *freshening* it, but abstained in her presence. The reporter declined his offer of coffee.

"It is tragic what happened to the Governor," the reporter began.

Lee W. nodded his head affirmatively, waiting for the real reason behind her presence.

"You were in on the surgery, as I understand. Quite a performance, Doctor Hickok." She paused, hoping for the man to offer more information on his own. Lee W. took a sip from his bourbon-less coffee and eyed the reporter.

"The vein of Leukowitz, I couldn't find it listed in Gray's anatomy."

Now she was getting to the point, Lee W. figured. Perhaps she just wanted to interview him for the same hero story that the Galveston paper was reporting. "Honey, you won't find it in a textbook. It is just a term we use here at UTMB."

Almost relieved, the reporter started asking other questions. "A cardio-pulmonary event claimed the Governor, is that right?"

Lee W. thought about the question. He took a long noisy sip of his hot coffee. He was not sure that this was a subject he should get into. "Well, we don't know at this point. Surgery is risky and people sometimes die."

"Is a pulmonary embolus a cardio-pulmonary event?"

Lee W. just stared at the reporter. He looked down at his sky-blue tie and picked an invisible piece of link off. He was not an expert on this issue, but he had a feeling that the reporter was right. A PE explained what happened to the Governor this morning. "Yes, a PE is in that class of event. But there are other causes like heart attack or stroke. We just don't know what happened at this point."

Harry put her backpack on the ground and removed a yellow tablet of paper. With pen in hand, she continued her questions. "Doctor Hickok, what are sequential compression boots?"

Now Lee W. was getting worried. Doctor Field's answer this morning in the Governor's room concerning them troubled him. These boots were standard in the care of the surgical patient, their lack perhaps fatal. Blood clots risks were a reality in that setting. "What was your name? Is it Jennifer?"

"Yes, Jennifer Harry from KTRK."

"Jennifer, those boots are something I am not an expert on."

"Did the Governor have them on at the time of his cardiac-arrest?"

Now Lee W. was worried. He hated to lie, but felt he had to. "I wouldn't know." Lee W. stood moving to the office door. "Yaw-all, I have patients to see."

The reporter apologized for taking his time. She stood and shook Lee W.'s hand. When he was alone Lee W. considered the woman's inquiry. As he thought his hand reached for the desk key. Quickly, he downed a shot of bourbon, adding the same *freshener* to his coffee.

CHAPTER 9
Autopsy

———⋀⋀⋀⋀———

For Doctor Luis Gomez, an autopsy was always an intellectually stimulating enterprise. When performed in the setting of a political death, it was downright thrilling. The autopsy that morning was the most important of his life. He performed hundreds of so-called posts, short for autopsies, during his career. While the thought disgusted the average person, for a pathologist it was exciting and produced satisfying final conclusions. Flipping through the medical record, he determined that Governor J.T. Splintter had a pulse-less cardiac-arrest after extensive pancreatic surgery. Despite exhaustive resuscitation efforts, including internal cardiac massage, the man unfortunately expired.

Luis stood in the autopsy suite dressed in a green scrub suit, his feet covered with surgical booties. He was of average height, a Latin America male, with bushy dark hair, brown horn-rimmed glasses, and a thin mustache.

Doctor Fields was unavailable and asked Lee W. Hickok to observe the autopsy. At the door to the morgue, the two friends met, shaking hands.

From the time of their UTMB residencies, Luis and Lee W. often socialized with their wives, Issa and Amber. These were good times, but they lost track of each other. They vowed to renew their friendship over beer, fish tacos, and bowling the following Saturday.

The UTMB Pathology department, which included the morgue, stood in the Ashbel Smith Building. The building was a ruddy colored historical building fondly called 'Old Red'. It was a Romanesque revival structure constructed of red pressed brick, Texas granite, and sandstone. It stood as a testament to Texas history, being the home to the first medical school west of the Mississippi. The first medical session opened on October 5, 1891, with just 23 medical students and 13 faculty. After several restorations, it was a beautiful historical and functioning building.

Luis led Lee W. to a refrigerated green tiled room, where the Governor's body lay on a stainless steel table. Lee W. placed stretchy surgical boot covers on his iguana skin cowboy boots, a paper gown over his street clothes, and disposable plastic gloves. Luis performed the autopsy while dictating notes through a headphone.

"A Rokitansky Y shaped incision was made to begin the procedure. This involved an incision beginning at both shoulders, splitting the sternum and dividing the abdomen in mid-line fashion. There was an existing left thoracotomy incision in the left fourth intercostal space which allowed access for internal cardiac massage. There was a well healing Chevron type, healing, upper abdominal incision."

Luis performed the autopsy as Lee W. watched. He questioned the pathologist throughout. His interests in the abdomen centered around the left renal vein. His two vascular clips placed on the vertebral vein were intact. He did not use the term Leukowitz, fearing that the pathologist might dictate that into the medical record. At its conclusion, the results appeared normal except for the following. "A large embolus was found totally occluding the pulmonary artery in a saddle fashion. Extensive ante mortem clots," that is pre-death clots, "were filling both lower legs and pelvis. No evidence of cardiac myocardial infarction, significant atherosclerosis of the cardiac arteries, or a cerebral vascular accident were noted. The tail of the pancreas and spleen were surgically removed. The liver showed some early signs of alcoholic liver disease."

The death diagnosis was massive pulmonary embolus or PE. Secondary diagnosis was deep vein thrombosis of the legs and pelvis. It was these clots which were the source of the pulmonary embolus. The pathologist commented on the absence of sequential compression boots, post-operative changes, and early alcoholic liver disease.

Dr. Gomez obtained microscopic slides for later examination. When examined they confirmed the preliminary results. Governor J.T. Splintter had died from a massive pulmonary embolus which originated in the deep veins of the legs.

•   •   •

Abbott T. Frankenstein loomed over his office window, studying his once flourishing kingdom with a deep, darkening scowl. It mortified him that the Governor died during his watch. His peptic ulcer reflected that feeling, burning dyspepsia in the pit of his belly tormenting the man. He opened his briefcase and chugged some liquid antacid from a large economy sized bottle, a recent unwelcomed addiction. With dejection, he sat heavily before his massive desk to think.

After much political haranguing, he successfully lobbied to bring the Governor to UTMB for pancreatic surgery. Texas is replete with fabulous medical centers, and bringing the executive to his institution was a coup. He had maneuvered and succeeded despite the University of Texas Austin Medical Center and the Scott and White Memorial Hospital in Temple, Texas, both of which had offered their services.

Then there was the actual competition: The Texas Medical Center. Located just north of Galveston in the greater Houston area, the medical center was the largest medical complex in the world with 15 hospitals and over 50 medicine related institutions. Doctor Michael DeBakey of that institution encouraged the Governor to have surgery in Houston. He was perhaps the world's most renowned physician; an innovator in cardiac surgery, scientist, medical educator, and international medical statesman. He removed the Shah of Iran's cancerous spleen in 1980 at the Maadi Hospital near Cairo in an event that some felt had something to do with the Iran hostage crisis. But in the end the Governor selected the quiet, idyllic Galveston; Frankenstein's greatest political coup.

The Governor was an alcoholic or nicely said to be a big drinker. It was an issue in his campaign for Governor, but Schlomo Goldine's shrewd political machine changed the title to social drinker. Still, the issue remained. Pancreatic pseudo-cysts occurred almost entirely in heavy, chronic alcohol drinkers. After his surprise election, he had experienced major medical problems and was in and out of the Austin Medical Center. The confirmation of the diagnosis did nothing but confirm the media's suspicion of alcoholism. Coming to the sleepy Galveston seaside was in part an attempt to escape large media attention of the Capital.

Frankenstein felt that the surgery was a fiasco. The President had his spies in the operating room, and truthfully the man was on his way to exsanguination when Lee W. Hickok stepped in. He was thankful at the time for providence's hand in the matter. The surgery's conclusion relieved the President, thinking incorrectly, that the worst was over and the powerful man would recover. His postoperative course, however, was a social nightmare. The Governor would not cooperate. He belittled the nursing and medical staff, refusing even the most basic instruction, springing the medical directive as a way around hospital policy. While Frankenstein refused to acknowledge the document, it was problematic, and contributed to a confusion on the ward. Incorrect decisions were made and one of those may have cost the Governor his life. Sequential compression boots were a standard of care in 1983. He did not much care about the life, but the death of the Governor in his institution would ruin his future political life.

He was waiting for the document when his secretary, Suzie, knocked on his office door quietly. She entered the room, as usual, intimidated by the enormous man. "Here is the report from Doctor Gomez concerning the Governor, Doctor Frankenstein. I have other papers for you as well." The woman whispered, placing a stack of charts and papers in his in-box. She turned and left the room, shutting the door quietly.

After another hidden swig of antacid, Frankenstein removed the three-page report and read silently to himself. Before him was the autopsy dictation, conducted just that morning on Governor J.T. Splintter. The final impressions confirmed his suspicions. It listed the cause of death as massive pulmonary embolus, which originated in the deep veins of the lower extremities.

Pulmonary embolism is a known complication after abdominal surgery. The cause has to do with stasis of blood pooling in large veins of the legs. After surgery these areas form clots which can break off and travel through the venous system, lodging in the patient's lungs. When massive as with the Governor, the embollus block the entire outflow of the heart and sudden death may occur.

Through the years, attempts were made to prevent blood clots, and pulmonary embolism in surgical patients. The first and most important maneuver is to get the patient out of bed and moving as soon as possible after surgery. In the Governor's case, little was done because of the patient's wishes and Schlomo Goldine's meddling. The second method of preventing these blood clotting issues was to mechanically compress the legs "milking" the blood out of the lower extremities. This was the idea behind sequential compression boots. Here they placed plastic wraps with air-driven chambers around the legs. An electrical pump then sequentially compressed and decompressed the boots resulting in the movement of blood. The third technique was to use anticoagulation to thin the blood. This technique was difficult in the post-operative patient prone to bleeding. Circa 1982-83 the state-of-the-art technique for preventing pulmonary embolus centered on compression boots and ambulation. The Governor had decided against them himself, Schlomo Goldine had sanctioned that decision, and together they may have just caused the man's death. Abbott Frankenstein would not allow disparagement of his Medical Branch; someone would have to take the rap.

CHAPTER 10
Anonymous Package

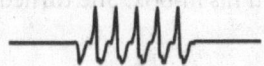

Jennifer Harry parked her rusting VW bug under a pepper tree and lugged her backpack up three flights of stairs, appearing for the first time in the KTRK newsroom in a week. They assigned her the Governor's case at UTMB. During the surgery she stayed in a cheap Galveston motel, while filing stories concerning surgery and death by the fax machine. The young reporter thought she was on to something big: complicity in the Governor's death revolving around the absence of a critical item of care, sequential compression boots. Everyone surrounding the events at UTMB was silent, however, an obvious sign of a scandal.

Jennifer planned to check in at the newsroom. She then would get home for a night off with a long soak in the tub, a good bottle of wine, and takeout Chinese food. Her first stop was the mail room, where she collected a stack of mail and memos, discarding the majority.

A manila envelope caught her eye. Addressed: Jennifer Harry, KTRK, Houston, Texas without a return address. Inside were papers stamped with the University of Texas Medical Branch logo. A three-page report stood out. Entitled necropsy, it was a copy of the Governor's autopsy report. Laced in medical terminology, the cause of death was clear: pulmonary embolism, the clot originating in the deep veins of the legs. The report commented upon the absence of sequential compression boots. Physician and nurse's hospital notes completed the package.

The packet just appeared in the mail, just recently mailed. It represented information vital to her. Someone at the medical center must have sent these. These stories indicated that the Governor was a very uncooperative patient. The documents confirmed that. They indicated that sequential compression boots, ordered by Doctor Fields, were often removed and not on at the time of death. It was the patient's wishes, and with Schlomo Goldine's compliance, they removed the preventative devices. The documents painted the entire story that she suspected and wanted to write. She would have to confirm this information somehow.

. . .

Dupree Harry was a 55-year-old African-American male patient of Lee W. Hickok. He was an upstanding Galveston citizen, a veteran, retired postal employee, active Boy Scout leader, and a man with the very common condition of prostate cancer. Seven years ago Lee W. performed a radical prostatectomy on Mr. Harry. The surgery removes the entire prostate and lymph nodes. The pathology from that surgery was disappointing in that it showed the spread of the cancer to pelvic lymph nodes. The presence of prostate cancer in lymph nodes implies that the patient is not cured, predicting recurrence. Despite this, he had done well.

The man considered Lee W. his primary physician. While the urologist encouraged him to seek a family practitioner, he always consulted Lee W. Lee W. liked the man, ordered tests and tried to take care of him. When he left a message for the urologist, Lee W. told his secretary to overbook an appointment that afternoon. It would be an appointment he would not soon forget.

Mr. Harry was sitting on the exam table when Lee W. walked in to see a man who had really become his friend. His prostate cancer tests were normal. They ordered routine tests for a 55-year-old man, his electrocardiogram and blood tests all normal. Lee W. met the man with a firm handshake. They made small talk about recent events and family and then got down to what was bothering him.

"Doc, I am really hurting all over and I been peeing red for a week!"

Lee W. listened and then examined the man. He helped the man to stand, which he did gingerly. The man slid done his sweat pants. What Lee W. saw startled him! Covering Mr Harry were dense bruises or ecchymosis across his abdomen, genitalia, and upper legs. Raised areas represented collections of blood or hematomas were present. One especially concerning area was over his left hip, very tender, the man shifting his weight off of it. Lee W. turned the man around. He saw an identical process over his entire back. The patient's examination startled Lee W. He had never seen someone so bruised. "What happened to you?"

Mr. Harry pulled his pants up and sat slowly on the exam table. "I got run over, Doc."

Lee W. thought for a moment with a confused expression on his face. "When was this?"

"Last week."

"Tell me what happened."

"I went out in the morning, Doc, to get my paper. Yaw-all know I live about two blocks from here. I been seeing you in the paper, by the way." He said with a big grin.

"Ya, but what happened to you?" Lee W. said, interrupting and bringing the man back onto the subject.

"I didn't see him coming."

"You got hit?"

"Ya Doc., run me right over that boy did."

Lee W. looked at the man. A boy had apparently run him over with a car. "What do you mean a boy?"

"That boy on a tricycle, he runs me right over."

There was a long pause as Lee W. realized the trauma that this man was talking about. The bruising that he witnessed was inconsistent with a low speed crash of a tricycle. Something was wrong with this man. Mr. Harry was in trouble. Lee W. started thinking about an abnormal bleeding condition called a coagulopathy. Here, proteins or factors in the blood involved in clotting are absent or reduced. The best example of this is hemophilia, an inherited condition.

"This bruising concerns me Mr. Harry. You say you have been having blood in your urine since that time?"

Mr. Harry shook his head affirmatively.

"Well, I think we need to put you in the hospital."

Mr. Harry said that that would be okay. "Is it the cancer, Doc?" The man said cautiously, respectful of the Doctor's knowledge.

Lee W. indicated that he did not know, but that it was a possibility.

They then admitted Dupree Harry to the hospital. Karen Green, the intern, came to write orders and do a history and physical. They ordered many lab tests, including an x-ray of the left hip. They asked the hematology resident on call to see the patient. Lee W. asked the intern to draw an extra red-topped tube of blood for a PSA.

PSA, or Prostate-Specific Antigen is a blood test that would revolutionize the treatment of prostate cancer in the 1990s; in 1983 it was only experimental. The protein is only made in the prostate, females, who do not have a prostate, have a zero level. Those men who undergo radical prostatectomy for prostate cancer if cured and free of disease should have a zero level. If in fact Mr. Harry had a coagulopathy caused by the spread of prostate cancer, his PSA would be very high.

Lee W. contacted a Baylor University Hospital colleague where the PSA assay was being studied. The Doctor agreed to have Mr. Harry's blood tested for PSA. They arranged a courier to take the blood the fifty miles from Galveston to Houston.

Hematology felt that Mr. Harry had a coagulopathy called DIC or disseminated intravascular coagulation. This is a condition where excessive clots form. The clots consume all the platelets and coagulation proteins resulting in bleeding. There are many causes of DIC, but the most relevant one is wide spread prostate cancer. The patient's x-ray of the left hip showed a hemarthrosis, a collection of blood in the joint.

After clinic, Lee W. and the others made hospital rounds. When they entered Mr. Harry's room they found him obtunded. An emergency CT scan showed a subdural hematoma, bleeding between the covering layers of the brain. Neurosurgery performed a burr hole to relieve intracranial pressure at the bedside.

In 1941, Doctor Charles Huggins first discovered remissions of wide spread or metastatic prostate cancer after surgically removing the testicles of patients with prostate cancer. That discovery won the Nobel Prize. This was a seminal discovery in the history of urology, for it revolutionized the treatment of this uniformly lethal form of disease. The response of prostate cancer to removal of the testicles is often dramatic. If in fact Mr. Harry was suffering from DIC caused bleeding secondary to spread of his prostate cancer, this hormone type therapy might very well resolve this.

After reviewing the case with hematology and neurosurgery, Lee W. said: "The thing is, Mr. Harry will die without some treatment of the DIC. The only thing that is treatable is if prostate cancer causes it, then hormone therapy might help. I think we should do an orchiectomy."

Here Lee W. referred to removing both testicles through a small scrotal incision.

"If the cause is not prostate cancer, he will die anyway." John Cooper added.

Obtunded and bleeding from DIC, Mr. Harry was in trouble. If in fact the cause of that was prostate cancer the procedure would shrink down the cancer and reverse the DIC. It would give him the greatest chance of recovery and resolution.

"We could do an orchiectomy under local in the OR. There would be a minor risk to him." Lee W. said.

All involved Doctor's agreed. As he was obtunded, he could not give his informed consent.

Karen Green grabbed the old chart from the ward clerk. In that chart was an advanced care directive. It designated a person to decide in circumstances such as this. The name listed in that document was Jennifer Harry.

• • •

The Jennifer Harry was in the newsroom when she received a phone call from UTMB. "A Karen Green is on the phone."

After introductions, doctor Green reported that Dupree Harry was deathly ill in the hospital. "Yes, I am his daughter," she said to the intern.

"He has a bleeding disorder that is very serious. It is likely from the prostate cancer. To treat him, we feel that a small surgery to remove the testicles is indicated. He is obtunded, however. He is not awake because of bleeding in the head. He is not competent to sign the consent."

"I can sign for him." Jennifer said. She recalled the advanced care directive that she completed a year before. She indicated that she could come to the University, perhaps arriving in an hour.

After obtaining consent, Mr. Harry is taken to the OR. Lee W. walked Karen Green through the surgery. Here, after the use of Novocaine, they made an incision in the scrotum. They then removed both testicles. There is minor blood loss from the procedure.

Lee W. went to the waiting room and found Jennifer Harry. It surprised him to find the reporter from his interview the other day. "Your Dad is very sick. He has a bleeding disorder called disseminated intravascular coagulation or DIC. We think this has been stimulated by the prostate cancer. We removed his testicles. That will shrink down any prostate cancer. If in fact the prostate cancer is causing the DIC, then it will resolve."

"How long will it take for the procedure to take affect Doctor Hickok?"

"That is a good question. I have seen people who the next day are better after this. Though this is an unusual case. Usually the procedure is done to get rid of bone pain, here we want bleeding to stop. I have seen people that take a month to respond. We hope for a quick result in your Dad because he has bleeding in his head."

"We will pray for him, Doctor."

The next morning on rounds Mr. Harry was sitting up in bed sucking on a glycerin swab.

"Mr. Harry, you are better already?" Lee W. asked. Jennifer Harry was sleeping in the bedside chair, and she woke up.

"Ya Doc. When can I get some food for breakfast?"

Jennifer Harry added: "yes he woke up last night. I think it is a miracle."

When he arrived at his office, a sticky paste-it note appeared on Lee W's door. It referred to a phone call from Baylor University in Houston. Mr. Harry's PSA is 3000 Ng/ml., 700 times normal. The theory seemed correct; the patient had DIC caused by prostate cancer and has responded to the removal of his testicles.

CHAPTER 11
Kon Tiki Room

—⋁⋀⋀⋀—

The Elephant's Ear Bar on Galveston's historic Strand was closing for the night. Lee W. was not done drinking, and the night was young. It was a problem, for 1 AM was the legal closing time for the city's alcohol establishments. Lee W. took his business elsewhere. He staggered past his parked Z car without recognizing it and ended up on Tremont St. where commerce was still booming.

The gigantic man with the shaved head met Lee W. on the sidewalk in front of an apparently closed establishment, the lights over the door turned off. He ushered Lee W. in through the front entry and returned to his position on the sidewalk.

A circus was in force within. Glaring neon lights, rotating spotlights, and a celestial mirrored globe rotated over a crowded cracked linoleum dance floor. Overhead roared raucous disco music from Donna Summer's greatest hits, echoing a booming beat. The floor was packed with men dressed in tight silk shirts with exposed chest and golden chains and flashy sequined women on stiletto heels and covered with heavy make-up.

Lee W. was startled, his ears burning from the overwhelming sound. A woman asked him for something called a popper, an ampule of amyl nitrite. He shook her off and moved across the crowded floor with difficulty to a long bar framed by a lengthy polished mirror. A handsome bartender with close-cropped hair and wearing no shirt was behind the bar. Shouting at the man, he asked for a double of Jim Beam. While he waited, he watched the mayhem. The song, YMCA, blasted and the entire room spelled it out with shouts and mannerisms. The song changed but its affect did not, sinuous movements between a man and woman, two men, or two women were present all over the floor, as they bounced to a gay beat.

His drink arrived with a small umbrella, and Lee W. paid with a healthy tip. A sip of the liquid revealed the farce. Cheap whiskey where Kentucky Jim Beam was needed. Lee W. tried to get the bartender's attention without luck. He decided to drink the inferior beverage.

A tap on his shoulder surprised the newcomer. Lee W. turned to face an enormous woman with a bleached blond wig, penciled on mole, long fake eyelashes, thick pasty make-up, a floor length red sequined gown, and platform heels. She smiled at the man, tasting her finger after placing it in his drink. "What are you drinking, sailor?" The woman laughed at the taste of the bad whisky. She whistled with her fingers and signaled to the same bartender. Soon an appreciated aged Kentucky whisky was in Lee W.'s hand.

"Thanks," Lee W. yelled over the blaring music. He took a long swig of his beverage, setting it down on the polished wooden bar after looking unsuccessfully for a paper napkin.

"What do you go by?" The woman said, placing something in his shirt pocket.

"Lee W.," the man yelled.

"Cute. Your darling," she said, grabbing his tie and pulling him to her.

Lee W. did not know what to say. The woman was really rather manly and ugly, especially at that distance. The woman let go. Lee W. took another swig, avoiding the plastic umbrella. "What is your name?"

"I go by, Eddie," she said. "Eddie Caruso, I own this joint. Never seen you here before, Lee."

Lee W. hated to be called just Lee, but declined to correct her. He was interested in her ownership. He had always wanted to own a bar. "Good for you, Eddie. Does it make a good buck?"

"You wouldn't believe it, Honey," she said with a wave of her wigged head.

Soon Lee W. was falling down drunk. The woman began to look better. He found himself dancing a disco jig on the crowded dance floor, the woman not the least bit intoxicated. She reached to the man and pulled him to her lips. Lee W. tried to turn his head and heard her whisper in his ear, " I still have a dick come back in a month my dear and I will take you around my new equipment!"

In the back room, a cocaine pile was on the glass mirror. Eddie used a razor blade and divided a portion into lines. Never before had Lee W. been around the powder. He hesitated, hoping that the woman would allow him to abstain. She encouraged him, and Lee W. snorted a single line. There was an intense burn in the back of his nose. His eyes were out of focus, and soon his nose ran with snot. His teeth burnt, his throat on fire. His heart beat as if it was out of his chest. Then a moment of pleasant mood slipped over him, not long-lasting but an apparent instant.

The music out front stopped. Whistles were heard. A siren coughed outside. Eddie looked frantic as she swept up the remaining powder into a brown paper bag. The toilet was exposed freely in the tiny room, and soon the material was flushed. A siren outside whelped out another signal as the woman pushed Lee W. through the front room and out the door. Once outside he put his head down and walked very inconspicuously along Tremont Street. The man with the bald head was on the ground tussling with two officers, hand cuffs out and shining. Police lights were flashing behind him as he turned the corner and practically fell on his Z car.

In the car he was out of breath. His nose was still running, and he was flushed and panicky. His ears were ringing, and he had a fierce headache over his blood-shot eyes. He preferred his heart within his chest; he decided A plastic umbrella was in his hand, and he dropped it to the floor as he fished his keys out of his pants pocket. Reaching to his shirt pocket, a business card spelled out the name of the club, Kon Tiki Room. The car was moving before he knew, and he slowly drove off.

CHAPTER 12
Alcoholic

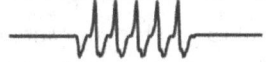

Lee W.'s secretary informed him of a 4 pm appointment with Doctor Frankenstein when he arrived in clinic the following day. All conflicting clinic patients were mysteriously cancelled, freeing up the time. Something was up and Lee W. was quite concerned. He finished his clinic and closed his office door behind him. A shot of Jim Beam was taken straight from the bottle. Two breath mints were placed in his mouth for good measure.

As Lee W. walked to the University President's office one thing stood out. While prior to the Governor's death the surgical success posters and banners celebrated, announcing that UTMB was Texas' Choice. Those signs were now gone. While they celebrated the success in an overdone fashion, the death of the Governor in the university was a tragedy, something that would haunt the medical center for years.

The prevention of post-operative pulmonary embolism was something that surgeons had wrestled with since the onset of general anesthesia. Stasis of blood flow in the legs and pelvic veins before and after surgery was a fact, and a certain percent of patients would have a thrombotic complication. Most felt that sequential compression boots reduced the incidence of clots in the legs. It was not a black and white thing, however. Those with the boots still had these complications, but the incidence seemed lower. Removing these in a patient after surgery does not guarantee a complication. In the Governor's case it just looked bad, especially how the staff was taunted by Schlomo Goldine. Over the next few weeks, discussion and debate concerning these facts would continue.

Lee W. arrived at the University President's office a few minutes early. Before walking into the suite, he popped a couple more of his breath mints, having a premonition regarding the substance of this appointment. Suzie, Frankenstein's secretary, offered him some coffee while he waited. She quietly congratulated Lee

W. for his success in surgery and then returned to her paperwork. She soon ushered him into the man's office.

Abbott Frankenstein and Lee W. met with a firm handshake. The president dressed in a blue seersucker suit, blue hand tied bowtie, and black wingtip shoes. Sitting quietly in the room's corner was the chief of urology, Fuad Fadi. Fadi looked very uncomfortable; his presence unexpected. Frankenstein encouraged the men to sit on his large leather couch while he pulled up a chair.

The president wasted little time getting right to the point. "I'll get right to it Lee W. We are all very thankful to you for your surgical skills with the Governor. Your insight into his problematic bleeding was right on, and you resolved the problem with keen insight." There was a pause while Frankenstein adjusted his bowtie. There was silence in the room and measurable uneasiness. "As I said, I will get right to the point. Were you drinking alcohol the night of the Governor's surgery?"

The question surprised Lee W. He looked at Fadi, who had his head down reading the carpet. That Frankenstein had the same information that Fadi had concerning his DWI was not surprising. The direction of the question caught him off guard. He wondered if a lie could cover up the fact that he had in fact been drinking; it was his only chance.

"If you are speaking of the DWI yes unfortunately, they stopped me on the way home from the hospital that night."

"Yes, that is unfortunate Lee W." Frankenstein said looking the man right in the eyes steadily. He stood and returned to his desk. Grabbing a sheet of paper, he returned and handed it to Lee W. "The police report from that night."

Lee W. stared at the document. Highlighted in yellow was the time of his arrest: 12:22 Am January 1, 1983.

"That arrest occurred soon after surgery, Lee W.!" Frankenstein folded his gigantic frame into the sitting chair next to the couch.

"Yes." Was all that Lee W. said.

"What was your blood alcohol level?"

Lee W. knew that the man had the information. "Zero point one eight." He said, adjusting his collar and noticing a bead of sweat on his neck. He wished his lawyer was present.

"Well, there is no question that you were drinking? That is not an equivocal blood alcohol level is it."

"No sir." Lee W. swallowed his breath mints.

"When did you consume the alcohol? And I'll tell you the truth, Lee W., there have been rumors for years that you drink while on call. Is that true?"

Lee W. was an honest man, but he was in a bind. "After the press conference I had some alcohol then left the University for home."

"Where did you get the alcohol?"

"I had two airline size bourbons in my desk."

"So you had what? These bottles are 50 cc's right."

Lee W. looked at Fadi while thinking. He really did not know. "I really don't know, Abbott."

"Well, yes they are 50 cc's so two would be 100 cc's. Did you leave the hospital right after that?"

"Immediately."

"Fuad," Frankenstein said, turning to the urology department chief. "Have you had any indication that Lee W. has been let's say under the influence during his years in your department."

Fuad Fadi was in a horrible spot. He was a friend to Lee W. Lee W. had lied to him. "Lee W. is an excellent urologist. I have had contact with him now, including his residency for what... how long Lee W."

"Six years of residency and five years here on staff. Eleven years Fuad." Lee W. looked the man in the eyes, hoping for some leeway.

"He has been nothing but an excellent physician. He is on time, trustworthy, his patient's love him, and he is excellent in the operating room." Fadi left his defense at that.

"Are you an alcoholic Lee W?" Frankenstein wondered.

Lee W. looked down at his now sad cowboy boots. He knew the answer but would not reveal it in this setting. "No."

Frankenstein looked at Lee W. He stood and moved to his floor to ceiling window and stood thinking for a moment. He returned and said: "Okay Lee W. I too have nothing but good things to say about your medical care. I have heard those rumors, however. Were you drinking that night, you know, before surgery?"

"No." Lee W. said again, looking the President in the eyes.

"Are you sure?"

Lee W. was aching inside. He reviewed that night in his mind. Could someone have seen him? He was certain that was not the case. Lee W. was silent as he looked up at the man. Frankenstein turned and walked to his desk. He opened a drawer and removed an object. He returned to the couch. Lee W. stood and moved slowly to Frankenstein's side. In the man's hand, was an airline size empty container of Jim Beam Bourbon. Lee W. said nothing.

"Frank Cercetti of OB Gyn was in the operating room that night Lee W." Frankenstein sat down waiting for the man's response.

Lee W. was white with fear. He reviewed the events of that night. When he entered the physician lounge, there were physicians watching television and others asleep on couches. Could one of those been Cercetti?

"He says he saw you drink this bottle. He retrieved it from the trash hamper."

Caught! If they knew how much alcohol he would be in even more trouble. Lee W. said nothing.

"That was just before the Governor's case. Could Frank Cercetti claims to have seen you drink this alcohol that night be true?"

"I did not see him in the OR that night."

"Believe me, he was there, and he saw you."

Lee W. looked down. He reluctantly shook his head affirmative.

"Did you drink the bourbon?"

"Yes." Lee W. admitted.

"What about that second airline size bottle when did you drink that?"

Here a lie would not do. He knew he was an alcoholic. It was time to stop the lies. Lying was part and parcel of alcoholism. The alcoholic must lie to continue drinking. He lies to himself. He lies to his loved ones. Lee W. could not lie anymore.

"I didn't just drink one other airline bottle. I had a bottle in my office." He looked down again at his boots. A tear came to Lee W.'s eye. He wiped it away slowly. He looked up at the president. "I was drinking before the case, Abbott."

Frankenstein looked at the man and slowly shook his head affirmatively. "Do you do this often?"

Lee W. wondered about his career. He only vaguely remembered his recent jaunt at the Kon Tiki Room. He had a good relationship with the President, but would his medical license be in jeopardy? Suddenly he missed his profession immensely. He had taken it for granted, but being a physician meant the world to him. "I drink every day, Abbott." Lee W. said with sadness.

"Are you an alcoholic Lee W.?"

There was silence in the room. "Yes." Lee W. said, looking down wretchedly.

"How much do you drink a day Lee W.?"

Lee W. wanted to be honest. He was embarrassed, however. He looked at Frankenstein. The man seemed sympathetic and had always treated him well. Could he be honest with the man? Lee W. yearned to do so. "I drink a lot Abbott."

"How much is a lot Lee W?"

Lee W. thought. Again he dropped his sight to the floor. "On a workday?"

"Yes. Take me through a typical day for you."

Lee W. never allowed himself to think about this subject. Absent-mindedly, he wiped his brow. "Well, I drink about a half of a 1.75 Liter bottle of Bourbon, a day. I know because I buy one about every other day. I drink wine at dinner. Maybe a few beers. But mainly I drink bourbon."

There was silence in the room. Frankenstein looked at Fadi and nodded to the man. Fadi excused himself. "I will leave you two alone." He stood and put a caring hand on Lee W.'s shoulder, then left the room.

"Thanks Fuad." Lee W. said, looking with embarrassment at the ground.

Again there was silence in the room. Frankenstein moved and sat beside Lee W. on the couch. "Lee W. do you get the shakes when you do not drink?"

The man thought of the weekend when he had abstained. He felt okay on Saturday, but by Sunday he was feeling poorly. Shaking, nausea, and a severe headache plagued him. In the end, he just treated those symptoms with a binge of alcohol drinking. "Yes."

"Well, it is dangerous to just stop drinking. We could put you in the hospital."

"No, definitely I won't do that. I'm too embarrassed. I'll be all right." Lee W. looked sincerely at Frankenstein. "Abbott, I am not sure I want to stop drinking."

"Well, that is a decision you will have to make. You must stop drinking in the hospital, however."

"Okay." There was a long pause.

"Lee W., there is a meeting of the physician's review committee chaired by Frank Cercetti tomorrow. You will be the prime topic."

Lee W. understood. Frankenstein called the shots, but the committee would decide on his future. "I understand Abbott." Finally, Lee W. stood and shook the President's hand.

Frankenstein put a hand on Lee W.'s shoulder. "Good luck to you, Lee W." He said as he closed the office door.

• • •

Lee W. found a closed up clinic when he finally made it back to his office. He unlocked the door, moved to his desk and drank a swallow of sweet amber. Sitting at his desk, he stared long and hard. Humiliation and some fright plagued him. Something that he had never thought would happen had just happened. Confronted with his drinking, caught with the truth of his alcohol use at work, the truth was so embarrassing. He had not always drank while on the job, but he had been doing so for quite some time. Caught now and by the university president, it was not an option anymore.

Alcohol was associated with many ruinous events in Lee W's life. Drinking was at the root of his divorce. Between his life in the hospital, and his drinking, he had missed so much of his only child's life. He had been unfaithful to his wife. Alcohol was not to blame for that one. He made a fool of himself so many other times, and always because of alcohol. He loved Amber and wanted to reconcile with her. She was adamant, however, not until he stopped drinking.

He weighed his options. Continuing drinking as before was not one of them. He had promised Frankenstein that he would not drink while in the hospital or on call. Continuing that practice would eventually result in severe ramifications. Could he continue to drink when not on call? He was not certain that he could, and besides, that would not satisfy Amber.

The solution to all of these problems was to stop drinking alcohol entirely. His prior attempts were so futile. He would be so sick, but that is what he needed to do. In-patient programs were available that had low mortality rates. Lee W. could not bring himself to that. He knew everyone around here and was too embarrassed to dry out in the hospital facilities. He had always thought he could get through the withdrawal by himself, using intravenous fluids and polypharmacy. He decided that night to stop drinking after one more binge, and self-treat his withdrawal symptoms.

CHAPTER 13
Hospital Evaluation

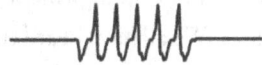

The conference took place in one of the meeting rooms on the fifth floor of the UTMB administration building. Here, long foldable tables and uncomfortable portable chairs complete with pitchers of cold water stood as a testimony to the situation. Coffee and styrofoam cups were available, the beverage produced in a large stainless steel urn on a side table.

The participants started filing into the room around the 10 AM scheduled time. Dr. Frank Cercetti was the chair of the physician's review committee, and by default was present. His involvement was key, having first hand involvement in the Hickok case. He was a balding grey haired man with rimless glasses, who always wore a hand-tied bowtie. He took his seat at the head of the table. Dr. Mark Fields attended and did so wearing his usual white coat over green scrubs. Dr. Nelson and Cromartie, the two attending anesthesiologists that night, entered through separate doors. They nodded to one-another, taking seats on opposite sides of the table. Dr. Fuad Fadi, the chief of urology, was in attendance. Madea Thomas RN was the operating room head nurse and was asked to speak for the operating room staff. Susie, Dr. Frankenstein's secretary, was present with a stenographer's tablet and a black ball-point pen to record the proceedings. The room filled in while Dr. Frankenstein pulled his frame onto a chair that looked juvenile for the man.

Cercetti welcomed the crowd. He indicated that the minutes would be taken down faithfully. He got right to the issue before the committee.

"On New Year's Eve night of this year we had the privilege of taking care of the late Texas' Governor. Surgery was indicated and performed by Dr.'s Fields and his staff. We'll hear later the details, but for the time let me just say that we meet today to evaluate a colleague who consulted that night on the Governor, namely Lee W. Hickok of the urology department."

"I'll start off. Now I was present in the surgeon's lounge that night. I performed a vaginal hysterectomy and was changing to go to my office. I witnessed Dr. Hickok as he took from his locker a small, what might be called airline size, alcoholic beverage and his consumption of that liquid. After his exit, I retrieved this bottle. Abbott I think you have that container."

Frankenstein removed the bourbon container from his white coat pocket and lay it on the table for all to see.

"Ya that was the bottle I retrieved that night. Let me just say that I have never witnessed the Dr. drinking before. We all have heard rumors, but I am saying today that I have never witnessed his consumption of alcohol at the University, that is before this event."

"Let's backtrack a bit. Mark you were in attendance that night. Tell us what occurred and how Lee W. got involved."

Attention then moved to Dr. Fields. "Well, J.T. Splintter came to us with a symptomatic pancreatic pseudo-cyst that he had been dealing with for quite some time. He elected to be explored at our institution, and Abbott could testify to the reasons for that. We explored him through a chevron incision, mobilized the tail and body of the pancreas with the pseudo-cyst. Unfortunately, we encountered a large amount of bleeding. It seemed obvious to me that the left renal unit was the source. I reached Dr. Hickok on the phone and asked him to consult. As you recall, all physicians were asked to take call from the house that night. He arrived soon after.

He viewed the Governor's CT scan and scrubbed into the case. With his direction, we dissected up the aorta and put a vascular tape around the left renal vein. With this we could see the source of bleeding, that is a vertebral vein that drains into the back of left renal vein. Lee W. placed two titanium vascular clips on the ends of that vein, and we controlled the bleeding. That was it. We completed the surgery, and the rest is history."

"Now Mark, were you aware of Lee W.'s alcohol consumption that night?"

"No, of course not. I've thought about it since, but in fact his surgical expertise impressed me. He showed no compromising condition at all."

"Had you heard of his alcoholism?

Fields looked down. He considered his answer. "I really had heard no rumors to that affect, myself."

"Ever operate with him before?"

"No, that was the first and only time."

Cercetti then turned to Dr. Nelson. "Mike, you did the anesthesia that night. Any problems with Hickok?"

"Never, and with this case he was prompt and from what I saw really did an outstanding job. I have, though, heard of his drinking. Never witnessed it except at a university sanctioned party."

Dr. Cromartie agreed with his colleague's description. He had never heard any rumors however.

"Let's get some nursing input," Cercetti said. "Madea, were you there that night?"

"No, I was at home and heard about it. Quite a performance, as I understand."

"In your dealings with the nursing staff, what can you add to our discussion?"

"Well, Dr. Hickok was really a hero that night according to all that I have heard. His drinking is known, yes. Not any first person contact I would say, but... people... would talk."

"What about his prior history?"

"Well, I go back a long time as you know," she said chuckling to herself. "When he was an intern, he was difficult to deal with. After that year, however, he has really cleaned up his act. I would say that I have never had a complaint since that first year. With me he has always been a gentleman. The nurses like him and respect his abilities."

"Abbott, any input?" Cercetti asked.

The man stood, stiff from sitting. He unfolded his long frame. "I have met with Lee W., and also Fuad. Lee W. is an alcoholic who has acknowledged that with us. He drinks here at the University often, however. My impression is that given the chance he would quit, pursue a 12-step program in Diversion. You never know with an alcoholic, but he has a chance to do this, and I think we should support him. Fuad, what are your feelings?" Frankenstein sat back down.

Dr. Fuad Fadi sighed before answering. "I know Lee W. from residency and his tenure here at the University since. He's good. He is an excellent surgeon and patients love him. I however, have let him down! I have heard about his drinking and have never confronted the man until this incident." The man shook his head and sighed again. "I should have taken him into my office and asked about the drinking rumors, but I did not. I should have helped him, but I did not. Gentlemen and ladies, I have let the university down concerning this. Abbott I offer my resignation."

There was silence in the room for several moments. Fuad Fadi was a man of unimpeachable character. He was the former chairman of surgery at the American University in Beruit. The staff idolized him, and his patients loved him.

Frankenstein spoke to the man. "Fuad if you are serious about this, but please we all looked the other way. We have a chance to do the right thing here. I ask you to reconsider."

Fadi thanked the man for his support. A tear was wiped from the corner of his eye. "My offer stands Abbott, but I thank you for your support. I would support Lee W. as well, and I hope that he will stop drinking and complete the program."

And so the committee offered Diversion to the urologist. This was a state-sponsored program of support groups and drug tests, which allowed the physician to continue to practice medicine. They proposed to have him withdraw from alcohol at the University as an inpatient for safety's sake. Little did they know that the physician was about to take this into his own hands.

CHAPTER 14
Bottle Caps

Lee W. admired himself in the floor-length mirror with a confident smile. He was naked, except for his red, white, and blue American flag engraved snakeskin-cowboy boots, which insulated his feet from the cold marble floor of his master-bedroom. He felt some relief, for he accomplished goal one, consuming a case of ice cold Lone Star beer, its demise represented by the empty Texas sized can dangling from his right hand.

A long sonorous belch escaped his mouth with a flourish. It began in his lower belly, echoing through his chest and mouth like a cannon blast, the rhythmic melody pleasing to the inebriated man. He tossed the empty can aside and wobbled down the hallway to the master-bath, kicking empties carelessly through the banister, each making a metallic clank as it crashed to the floor two levels below.

Lee W. opened the bath's door carefully, aware of fragile bottles sitting on the floor like pirates-loot. He flipped on the wall switch, lighting the room with a glaring bare bulb hanging from exposed electrical wires. At his feet sat goal number two, dozens of gleaming, assorted, premium, alcoholic beverages, gathered during a rouse of his home, waiting for consumption.

He ran a warm bath, adding a pinch of bath salt to the claw-legged tub. He bent to remove his boots. However, the abdominal bloat and blood alcohol level made this impossible. He thought about his situation for a moment, dismissed the need to remove his boots, and stepped carefully into the partially filled tub. Sitting, he slipped to his backside with a splash, his boots now filled with warm soapy water.

On the floor before him sat his objects of interest, formerly worshiped glass bottled beverages arranged in no particular order. He gathered the group meticulously from every nook and cranny of his home, collected from the years of his prolific drinking. He raided vigorously his great room, kitchen, dining room, three bedrooms, bathrooms, basement, and garage. Before him lay bottle after bottle of containers labeled Gordon's, Jameson, Smirnoff, Johnnie Walker, and Jose Cuervo. Fifths, liters, handle sized containers, wine bottles, airline bottles, and hip flask pints were all represented.

Goal number two was to drink all this alcohol in one sitting. He began by examining his horde, selecting a particularly fine fifth of Johnnie Walker for his first taste. He broke the seal with a brisk twist of the cap and started on what until now had been his favorite pastime. A third of the bottle was gone when he noticed that pouring the rest over his head and body might facilitate the task.

He handled bottle after bottle the same way. With interest he would select a beverage, snap it open, and throw the cap onto the bathroom floor. He would drink till he had lost interest and then pour the remainder over his intoxicated body.

This process went surprisingly quick, for Lee W. was until that point in his life a prolific drinker. Bottles were cast aside, scattered across the floor, some stacked against the bathtub's porcelain wall. Soon just a taste of the liquor and then the majority of each bottle was poured in the tub, overwhelming the tiny drain, the reservoir becoming filled, as with an expensive alcohol bubble-bath. An inadvertent wipe of his face with the back of a hand, and his eyes were stinging with tears. Water from the spigot helped. The smell overwhelmed the small room, a very strong, overpowering medicinal alcohol smell. Lee W. felt rejuvenated, fresher and cleaner than ever before.

A deep alcohol induced sleep enveloped the man, interrupted only when his head would drop for a moment below the surface of the water. He would gasp, cough violently, reposition himself, and continue along in dreamlike bliss. Gradually Lee W. awoke, aware that he had accomplished his second goal.

Even while inebriated he could finish his housekeeping chores, for Lee W. could hold his liquor. He bagged all the discarded bottles and beer cans and placed them on the curb for the garbage man. It was painful to discard so many years of pleasure. Lee W. loved to drink and had done so liberally since his teenage years. His Dad and his Dad before him drank, and Lee W. continued the pattern with thoughtless passion. He had seen good times and bad, peaceful and violent, quiet and loud, and throughout those times, like a good old friend, he had drink. He was finished, however, except for this one last binge. It was quite a loss, all that booze gone, much of it down the antique bathtub drain, and as Lee W. sobered up he felt sick to see it all go. He had to rid his house however, for if he just discarded the plunder, placing the bottles at the curb for the trash collectors, some kid might get his first taste of whisky, or more likely he would go out in a delusion and retrieve it. He had to quit drinking, that was all there was to it.

He sat gloomily at his kitchen table pondering his next goal; the cessation of alcohol consumption and withstanding the inevitable withdrawal. Alone with his bottle of aged Kentucky Jim Beam, his preferred beverage, he wondered if he would ever stop. Fingering the bottle lovingly, he realized that he may never have another. With some sadness and deliberation, he broke the seal and opened his last bottle. He poured himself a double in his favorite glass tumbler. He slung it down, the burn so recognizable and familiar. Soon there was a second drink, then a third. The buzz was in force and sooner than he had imagined. Shortly he was pouring another and then another as the Saturday became thick and black. The last thing he remembered were thoughts of Amber, sweet and petite.

CHAPTER 15
Schlomo

———————/\/\/\/\\———————

The Galveston sun peaked through billowy January clouds, as Schlomo Goldine, in the lime-green suit, was wheeled to the black limousine by the nursing assistant. He was a mess; hair standing up, bald head uncovered, tie twisted, and collar askew, but his small black cowboy boots were recently shined. The woman locked the wheelchair at the side-walk, attempting to help the man to his feet.

Schlomo spit: "Get away!" He brushed the nurse aside and climbed into the car, slamming the heavy car-door behind him. The nurse waved sarcastically, as the Lincoln Continental with the prominent roof antennae sped away with a skid.

Showing no patience, Schlomo whipped shut the darkly tinted side windows. He picked up the intercom and barked orders at the driver.

"Hobby and make it quick!" He referred to the Governor's private plane, which sat on the south Houston tarmac. "For once hurry man!"

The driver, in a black short brimmed hat, glanced at his passenger in the rearview mirror with disdain. Silently, he flicked off the intercom switch and sped up. With one hand he lit a cigarette with the car-lighter and blew smoke out of the crack of the window. He shook his head quietly, as if treated similarly many times before.

The Chief of Staff was furious. He was overwhelmed by the attempted resuscitation of Governor Splintter, an unwilling witness to a violent, sudden death. Never had he seen such a traumatic and chaotic scene. This bloody act was sure to haunt him for years. Schlomo felt certain that he himself had suffered a heart attack and was incredulous about the treatment. He did not faint. The incompetent medical staff created the diagnosis at UTMB. Cretins, morons, they were everywhere. He would collect victims in the future, he decided.

A fold down mirror was produced from the back of the seat, and Schlomo gave all of his attention to his thin hair. He shook his head, dismayed by his disheveled appearance. Reaching to a duffel-bag, he produced a can of hairspray. After gently collecting strands of hair over his balding head, the spray was used profusely until empty. The aerosol filled the back seat space like a nasty cloud. When finished, Schlomo tossed the can to the floor, coughing several times. The flap of hair was then secured to his scalp with wads of wax. He replaced the mirror after a long examination, smiling proudly to himself, kicking his boots with glee.

Schlomo removed his gold embossed clip board from a red stripped leather briefcase. He read silently, making marks and scribble with a gold ball-point pen, having a pink ball of fuzz on the end. A citizen's band (CB) radio mounted on the floor squawked. Schlomo quickly picked up the receiver attached to the long coiled cord. He listened carefully.

"This is easy rider coming on down in the Baboon Butt. I-45 is history. In need of a Tommy, any info out there?" The truck driver spoke through the CB using trucker lingo. He indicated he was driving I-45 in a Kenworth truck and needed fueling.

"Tiny Dancer here. I have a Smokey report. There's a bear in the grass in an astronaut advertising," Schlomo replied using his handle. He reported sighting a policeman in a speed trap. "Smokey's got a customer." Indicating that someone was stopped by the officer. "Going ten-ten."

Schlomo replaced the microphone. He picked up his clipboard, checking off items with his pen. He turned his head and stared out the window. Todd Franco was his assistant in Austin. A catholic practicing man, Schlomo gave him a handle that reflected his religion. Picking up the microphone, he spoke over the airway.

"Come back, Monk. Tiny Dancer here," Schlomo reported. Squawk... "Ya, this is Todd," the voice said unenthusiastically. "Your handle: Monk!!!! Never speak your name fool!" Schlomo lectured.

"Ya, Ya ... come in... Okay come in boss."

"Monk your attitude! Info on Big Daddy's demise? Comeback." Much had happened. Austin would hum over the Governor's death.

"Well, the media is buzzing. Rumor is that he died from a, what do they call it? A PE, pulmonary embolus. I just got the autopsy report. Turns out those boots were vital boss... err Tiny Dancer."

"Big Daddy insisted on their removal. Don't those vultures know I was just following orders! Come back."

"Get this! Turns out Hickok was drunk as a skunk. I have the DWI police report. Ah... come back."

"What!! He was drinking? But he certainly was sober during the surgery?" Schlomo's mood picked up suddenly. Under the clipboard was his discarded water-soaked business card, still in place. He flipped its edge with his thumb.

"I don't think so. Surgery ended at 12:03 AM. He was ticketed just 19 minutes later with a 0.18 blood alcohol level. He was drinking before surgery!"

Schlomo's wheels turned. A sinister expression came over the man. If he was anything it was vindictive. The Governor died because he had removed the boots. They needed cover, and that urologist disrespected him. He will be the fall guy, he decided with an evil smile. A menacing plan formed in his mind. Hickok would take the blame. No one would fault the Governor's hand chosen chief of staff, the political genius. Schlomo raised the microphone to his mouth as the limo pulled up and stopped on the tarmac. "This is Tiny Dancer 10-7," Schlomo said, signing off.

• • •

Kegan Macintosh was a lifelong journalist who felt slighted. He was a redheaded man with a ginger complexion, slightly overweight prune-like body, who continually pulled up his pants. He never got the *big* break or rocketed to fame, as was his destiny. He moved around frequently, occasionally fired, transferring from paper to paper looking for that one chance, always just a small city reporter. He was a loner, even in high school where his work on the campus paper was overlooked. It was the same story at the Austin American Statesman. He had campaigned for the Galveston duty, following the little-publicized Governor's surgery. He knew Goldine from before. Assigned to the Governor's entourage, he felt that his relationship with the chief of staff might benefit him. With Splintter's death, that hope was dashed. The man just died. Schlomo Goldine was out of a job and influence. He wrote up his article on the Governor's demise, and returned to Austin, when a phone call changed everything.

"Macintosh." Kegan responded to a phone call when he arrived at his cluttered American Statesman desk.

"You don't know the facts," a voice said matter-of-factly.

"Who is this?"

"You don't want to know. Just figure out who killed the Governor."

"Who killed? He died of a blood clot."

"Ah, but who is responsible?"

Kegan thought for a moment. Was there something to the rumors? "Who?"

"Look to the Galveston police. There was an arrest. You will have to find out yourself!" Click the phone went dead.

Kegan took a sip of cold coffee sitting on his desk since before the Galveston trip. It was bitter and contained a dead fly. He spit a mouthful into the paper cup. What did he have here? His intuition suggested a big story. The call was untraceable. What kind of arrest was the voice talking about? His source in the Galveston police would have to snoop around.

"Melvin? Kegan Macintosh here." He wasted no time and made a phone call.

Melvin was a desk-bound want-to-be in the police force on the island city. He was helpful to a point; the point being cash for information, but this was important.

"An arrest. There was an arrest about the time of the Governor's operation?"

Melvin knew. It was all around the station. He would cough it up for a fresh Franklin. "Ya, what's it worth?" Kegan and Melvin were on the same wave-length.

"A hundred in a plain envelope at our usual drop." Kegan would mail the bill to the reporter. Two days later a trip to the post office yielded the bill. He was on the clock and driving a black and white, clearly violating his job description. He stopped at the bar, *Second Amendment,* for a drink, which became several. He would wait for Kegan.

The call was immediate on his return to the station. "Who are you referring to?" Kegan said.

"Hickok of course."

"How is he involved?"

"A DWI that night."

"Well it was New Year's eve. Big deal."

"Big deal? Big deal? He was drunk in the OR!"

"Wait... what?"

"He's a drunk. He was definitely legally drunk during the surgery!"

"He drank after surgery, come on." Kegan was believing the story. He too had heard the rumors of Hickok's drinking. He was playing the devil's advocate with Melvin.

Melvin laughed quietly. "No man, he was high in the operating room. Figure it out. Surgery ends at 12:03. The man is picked up at 12:22 with a 0.18 BAL. Do the math. No one can blow that level after just 19 minutes of drinking!"

There was silence on the phone. Kegan began crunching the facts. A drunk surgeon and the patient dies. Culpability is obvious, at least on a non-legal media level. What a story. He saw himself becoming syndicated worldwide. "I need the police-report!"

"Going to cost you another two Franklins!"

"Have it in the box by sundown!" Kegan slammed down the phone.

CHAPTER 16
Delirium Tremens

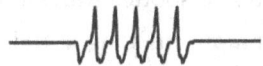

The grey sky broke over the waves of the gulf as he awoke; a biting wind blowing sand from the east. A curious seagull picked at his red-white and blue boot a yard up the beach. Others flew above, caws tossed down for their inquisitive peer's encouragement. He lay on his face, an impression made in the moist sand. A blue Dallas Cowboys sweat shirt with the hood pulled up over his head and a worn pair of jeans covered him. In his hand he grasped an empty bottle of Jim Beam, perhaps one swallow left drying in the bottom.

In the burgeoning sunlight, Lee W. opened his one uncovered eye and stared at the surrounding sand. He sputtered some debris and swallowed with a parched tongue. He let go of his bottle and turned slowly over onto his back, spitting thick mucus out at nothing. He sat slowly, each hand bracing and dragging in the sand.

Lee W. looked at the waves for the longest time, his mind numb and blank, wondering how he had gotten to this place. The surf crashed and crashed, its rhythm timed to the pulsing of his aching head. Soon bits of the night returned to his encrusted mind. The empty bottle, his position on the east end beach, his one tossed boot; all seemed consistent with his stained memories. He remembered the bathtub, and his last bottle of Sweet Amber. He swam that night in those crushing waves, clothed in his boxer shorts. He then shivered until dry and dressed again quickly. Shouting and singing returned to his mind, like pieces of driftwood thrown into the surrounding surf.

Beyond that, the night was a blank, his first memory tossing out the alcohol supply and sitting at the kitchen table. His intention at the time was that this would be the one last night, and by his surroundings and the nauseous feeling in his gut he had succeeded with the blacked out binge portion of the deal. He had accomplished his three goals.

Lee W. stood unstably and hobbled down the beach, chasing the seagull away to retrieve his boot. Standing on one leg, he wiped debris from his nearly dislodged sock, replacing the boot. He picked up his bottle, slugged the last drop and tossed it with a crash into an open barrel full of rotting trash, as seagulls scattered away. He made his way slowly up the beach, climbed the rocky embracement and crossed the seawall.

Standing now at Jill's Diner, he glimpsed himself in the window's reflection. His beard was an unkempt stubble, spotted with sandy debris. Lips were parched, the upper split from dehydration, his tongue trying desperately to mend the situation. A large swollen, bruised abrasion was evident across the right forehead. His eyes were thick and red with a watery discharge and one sub-conjunctival hemorrhage. Under his hood were several inch pieces of drying seaweed, which he dislodged by pulling down the covering. His hair was plastered to his face, the back sticking up like dark brown cotton candy. Lee W. took in the reflected image and etched it in his mind. He tried to freshen his hair with his hands and dislodged sand from his face, sweat shirt and drying pants. He kicked pieces of seaweed off of his beloved red, white, and blue boots, before slowly moving on into the diner. The clanging of the bell as he entered pierced his aching head. He sat with a thud at the counter and whispered the usual to the hostess.

The waitress stood looking at Lee W. with a question in her mind. "Yaw-all look like shit, Lee W." An uncomfortable silence filled the room. "Should I liven that up?" She said as she poured a cup of black coffee for the disheveled man and pulled a bottle of brandy from behind the counter.

Lee W. put a hand over the cup and whispered: "No, Honey."

"What happened to your head?"

Lee W. did not look at the woman; he just stared down at his steaming cup of coffee. He reached to his forehead and felt the abrasion. "I don't know." Was all he said, his voice cracking. After the woman moved to prepare his usual, he hastened to the restroom. Once inside the stall he lifted the seat and violently vomited. After washing his face, he stared into the mirror with horror, the toil of ethanol visible to the world. He reached into his right shirt pocket and grabbed a prescription bottle, setting it down for the room to read. While still examining himself in the mirror he removed its child-proof cap, picked out the bundle of cotton, and shook two pills into his parched mouth. Reaching down with his hand, he scooped water and swallowed hard.

At the counter his usual, eggs and grits were waiting for him. He sat and stared at the unappealing congealing mass. After a few bites he left a five and slowly moved out, saying nothing. The medicinal effects took hold as he walked the three blocks to his home. At the porch, he realized he did not have any keys. Turning the knob, he recognized that the door was unlocked.

Inside, the chaos startled him. In the great room a lamp was turned over, pads from the couch scattered across the room. Chairs were cast over in the dining room as if a séance had ended on a bad note. The refrigerator door was open, melting ice covering the floor. A hole in the entry wall matched the abraded sore over his right forehead and soon he recalled further elements of his last night.

Lee W. moved to the open refrigerator. Standing in the melted ice, he grabbed a bottle of Pedialyte, his favorite the purple grape flavor. He then drank liberally until his stomach could hold no more. Turning, he climbed the stairs slowly to his room, the purple bottle in his hand. He then fell on to his waterbed with a crash.

When he awoke he was shaking. Lying on his face again, he watched his hand as it shook back and forth, knowing it was time. His head was on fire, a pulsating, throbbing pain that tried to push out his eyes. In the pit of his stomach was a crashing feeling, rumbling and cramping lightly in pain; the beginnings of nausea evident. His muscles ached, beginning with his arms and finishing with his feet.

Lee W. sat slowly on the firm edge of his waterbed frame. He tried to move with deliberation, the waves of the bed a bit much for the man. He reached in his shirt pocket and removed the prescription bottle, placing it on his nightstand. Percocet, an oxycodone containing oral pain medicine set for the room to read. He reached to the floor and pulled a large brown grocery bag on the bed next to him. He removed two other prescription bottles, placing each next to the first; Compazine for nausea and Librium take three times a day for anxiety typed on the labels. Then a large bottle of thiamine, vitamin B, was placed on the nightstand. Liter bags of intravenous saline were removed and tossed to lie on the floor by the wall.

He then stood slowly and grabbed a metal wire hanger from the closet. Sitting back down he fashioned himself a hook, attaching one end to the IV bag, the other slung over the bed headboard to hang. Next he took IV tubing and plugged it into the IV bag. Opening the stopcock, he flushed the tubing on the floor. He removed several IV needles and placed them on the nightstand. After removing his sweat shirt, a tourniquet was applied to his left arm. With shaking hands he was able to start the IV on the first stick, attaching the tubing and letting a half liter flush into his vein. He then turned the IV rate down. Next, a disposable emesis basin was produced from the bag. He then promptly vomited into the yellow plastic container. He then opened each prescription with his shaking hands. He succeeded in swallowing two percocet, one Librium, one compazine, and three thiamine each one after the other. He washed down the pharmacy with a big swig of Pedialyte.

After vomiting he felt a little better, and he dropped to his back, looking up at the circling ceiling. He was sorry at that moment for the waterbed, for the slow waves magnified in his aching head. He assessed his situation. He was hooked up to an IV that at this rate would last for several hours. If he could keep from vomiting, the percocet, Librium, compazine, and thiamine would last as well, hopefully making his withdrawal tolerable. Now, if only he could go to sleep.

•   •   •

The tiny room was lit by the full moon, rays cascading through the torn red curtains giving a bloody hue. Through the closed door he could hear them at it again. Yelling and screaming had awakened him, a phenomenon that was unfortunately common of late.

When the loud crash occurred, he knew he had to move and witness the tainted scene. He crawled out of his single bed with his bear Ben in his hand, scrambling across the dark room and reaching up to open the door. Moving down the darkened hallway, the yelling increased in intensity. It was one-sided, a loud male voice dominating the frightening conversation. At the edge of the room, he stood and watched the two. They had turned a bookcase over, and the man was threatening to hit the woman who already had the beginning of bruising on her tear-stained face. When they saw the boy, they both yelled for him to return to his room, using his formal name Lee Wiley. The woman was crying and picking up the fallen books. The man was standing threatening her with a bottle in his hand.

He moved to the man, shaking his hand and throwing his bear. The man laughed at the boy, pushing him down like a matchstick. The man took a swig at his bottle and wiped his mouth slowly. He stepped over the boy and moved to confront the woman.

The boy looked up with fright at the huge figure, hate quickly replacing the fear. The woman rushed to his side, gathered him up with his bear and pulling him down the hall to his tiny bedroom.

In the car, his Mom said they would be safe at Grandma's. She put Lee W. in the back seat and told him to hold on tight to Ben. When she tried to start the car, you could see her say a silent prayer, the battery of the ancient sedan often dead. The engine caught, and the two moved out. His Dad ran out of the rundown house when the car started. He tried to stop them, throwing a pack of cigarettes as he tried to force open the car door and flag them down. Lee W. watched over the front seat as they disappeared into the dark.

At the intersection, the bright headlights bared down on them from the driver's side before the impact. With the blaring sound of tires on pavement, the two cars hit, the force throwing the boy into the back seat. He always remembered his Mom dead and lifeless, cast about in the front seat before him, the hysteria as he realized what had happened, and the crazy attempts at revival.

The dream was not a new one, but its real life texture was. What had happened now forty years ago had tormented him, but tonight's dream with the withdrawal of alcohol was so much more authentic and troubling. His Father, in a drunken stupor, caught and T-boned them in that intersection, his Mother dead on arrival. It changed forever his life, living during his upbringing with his drunken, abusive father.

Lee W. shook off the anxious feeling that always accompanied the dream. His head was still piercing with pain behind his eyes. Soaked now with sweat and shaking with cold, his hands became especially tremulous. His body ached from the tip of his nose to his feet. He reached for more medicine but was unsuccessful.

·   ·   ·

She arrived as an angel, somehow immediately in the room and comforting him.

"Honey, what are you doing?" Amber wondered as she assessed the room and her new patient.

Lee W. lay on his back, his left hand attached to an empty IV bag draped over the side of the bed. He was wet with sweat, and shivering. A black and blue abrasion was visible over his right forehead. Dressed in an old wife beater sleeveless T-shirt, it was pulled up at the waist, his belly showing. Levi pants were open at the waist, boxer shorts pulled high over the fly, one sock missing from his left foot. The room was in chaos. The bed sheets were torn up, loose on all corners exposing the underlying waterbed mattress. On the nightstand a lamp without its lampshade, an emesis basin full of vomit, scattered prescription bottles, and an empty pedialyte bottle could be seen. Along the wall were IV bags, cowboy boots, and a wadded up Dallas Cowboys sweatshirt. The room reeked of vomit, emesis stains on the sheets, shirt, and sweatshirt.

"Lee W, are you all right?" Amber said as she sat on the side of the bed and shook his face gently. "What are you doing?"

Lee W. opened his eyes. He tried to focus on Amber but had difficulty due to the nystagmus in his eyes. "Goal number four, stopping drink." Was all that he could say.

Amber looked at the IV bag. She pulled it from the headboard and changed it. With the IV now running she carefully took the emesis basin into the hallway, dumped it into the bathroom toilet, and returned with some dry towels to clean him up.

She then examined the prescriptions on the nightstand. Percocet was for pain. She knew he must be in horrible pain. The Compazine for nausea. She had seen the results of that. However, the Librium and thiamine seemed the most important. He was in the middle of alcohol withdrawal and Librium was a benzodiazepine, the class of drug used to replace alcohol in these types of cases. Thiamine or vitamin B1 was deficient in many alcoholics and withdrawal seizures, and other neurologic disorders related to this deficiency were seen. She decided then to keep him dosed with Librium and thiamine.

Before that, another subject needed to be discussed. "You need to go to a hospital, Lee W.!" She was not familiar with the one third incidence of mortality with alcohol withdrawal, but knew that his life was at stake.

Lee W. seemed to improve for this brief interchange. Grabbing the woman's hand he said. "No Amber, please. I can't go to the hospital. Not now. I know everyone. I am too embarrassed. Please promise me you won't call for an ambulance!"

"Honey, you could die here."

"I don't care. Please don't take me to the university!" Amber thought it out as she cleaned up the man. If Lee W. was to die, she would be held responsible. She would have to watch him closely and if he got worse, she would have to overrule his wishes. She moved to the bathroom, retrieving a thermometer. She decided to document his vital signs at least every hour and took his temperature of 101 degree Fahrenheit. His blood pressure was measured at 190/90. Then she dosed him on the Librium and thiamine, hoping that he could keep these two important meds down.

Lee W. looked at Amber with frightened, bulging eyes. Lifting the sheets he said: "there's bugs in these sheets, Amber!" The man sincerely believed this and was terrified.

Amber looked at the sheets carefully but concluded that there were no insects. She did not know these were tactile hallucinations, or so-called formication, common in alcohol withdrawal. For Lee W., Amber's assurance seemed to calm him.

Amber went downstairs to the answering machine. 25 messages had gone unanswered, including many of hers and several from the clinic at the hospital. The first of these was five days earlier. She concluded then that Lee W. may have been self- treating his withdrawal four to five days. She made a phone call to the university clinic telling them that he would be gone another week. She made similar arrangements with her employer.

Upstairs Amber straightened up the room. She replaced the lampshade and sprayed down the room with Lysol. Lee W's T-shirt was so soiled with vomit that she cut it off with band aid scissors and tossed it in the trash. She took warm water and towels and cleaned Lee W. up, and got him into the bed now made up with new sheets and blankets. She got a Librium and a few thiamines, got Lee W. sitting up carefully to swallow the medications. His tongue was swollen and parched, but with pedialye he could swallow them. She lay next to Lee W., kept track of his vital signs, watching his IV, medicating him, and comforting him when he had hysterical dreams.

The following day she could get some chicken soup down the man. His tremor seemed better and his temperature became normal. Soon the IV was taken out, as his liquid intake increased and supported him. She got Lee W. into the tub, wondering about the nearly forty alcohol bottle caps scattered across the floor, and then helped him shave. The next step was to help him down the stairs to the kitchen where she could cook meals for him.

When he asked her to liven up his coffee, Amber did not know whether or not he was kidding. Lee W. did not smile, but stared at the coffee and then at the woman herself.

"Yaw-all can't drink anymore!" Amber said as she touched his arm with tenderness.

Lee W. shook his head affirmatively, and then put his head on the table for a moment. "I am glad I don't drink anymore, but it is so tempting. I still feel like shit. Amber," he said, grabbing her arm. "Thank you for helping me. How did you know?"

"I called you maybe 10 times and yaw-all never answered. So I drove over. I could tell what you were doing. You looked like Hell. I just had to help you."

Lee W. took a good sip from the coffee cup. He decided he liked the taste more without the brandy. But still in his bones he desired the alcohol.

"Where is all your alcohol?"

"I got rid of it except for one last bottle of Jim Beam. I drank it pouring some down the drain. It took at least an hour," the man underestimated.

"What did you do with that last bottle?"

"I drank it, Saturday I think. Woke up on the beach. Then I came home and fell asleep for a long time. I was in DT's when I awoke. So I medicated myself and put in an IV. The next thing I remember is sweet Amber arriving like an angel and saving me."

"You saved yourself, you big lunk." Amber said rustling up his hair. "Why did you do this Lee W?"

"My drinking just can't go on. Frankenstein has proof that I drank before the Governor's surgery!" Lee W. said, leaving the statement to stand for itself.

"What do you mean proof?"

"Frank Cercetti saw me down an airline bottle of bourbon that night in the physician's lounge and even recovered the bottle for Frankenstein. What a friend. Then they know about the DWI. So I was told I must not drink on call again. But you know what; alcohol has dominated my life for the last maybe 20 years. It killed my mother. You divorced me, Kellie hates me. It just seemed like the time to stop."

"You know that I support you with this. But drinking is not the only thing. Lee W. Your anger and then the adultery. I don't know if I can forgive you for that."

"I will stop Amber. You will forgive me, won't you? After I recover and am back at work I will work through these things. I want you to know Amber that I love you and will forever. That girl, so foolish, it won't happen again."

"You need to go to AA, Lee W."

Lee W. looked down at the floor. He then took a sip of coffee. "I don't think I need that."

"You are going need support. I want you to! AA saved my daddy! Look... I looked in the phonebook there is an AA meeting on Friday night."

"I will think about it, Amber."

CHAPTER 17
Jennifer

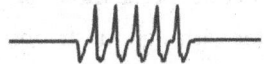

The rain poured for a second windy day of tropical depression Patrice. Galveston was in its path, a frequent victim to gulf coast storms. She had the red VW bug flying across the causeway, windshield wipers too small and feeble to really do much. For years the beetle leaked in these storms, and Jennifer Harry's tennis shoes were wet from standing water in the car's bottom. She was used to this, and she shifted gears with little thought.

On the island, I-45 becomes Broadway, the poorly leveled street now with curbs full of standing water. At Fourth Street she made a left, parking on Mechanic in a puddle. Opening the door revealed a literal pond of dirty water swelling to the door, and she jumped from the car, still getting soaked. She reached in her leopard pattern backpack, produced a small matching umbrella, and ran towards the medical center.

They crowded the old John Sealy reception area with people seeking a breather from the storm. The teenagers were listening to Walkmen and wearing stretchy surgical hats, as was the odd style. She waited for the elevator, thought against it and took the stairs climbing two at a time. The urology offices were on the second floor, and she snuck past the receptionist. Trying a back door, she found herself in front of Dr. Hickok's office. She knocked on the closed door without a response.

"Can I help you?" The young nurse asked.

Jennifer turned and grimaced, now caught someplace she shouldn't be. "Is Dr. Hickok here?" She wondered, turning on a big friendly grin.

"No. He is gone for this entire week. His health; something about being sick."

Jennifer felt concern. Her father, Dupree Harry, was just discharged from the hospital. She wondered where the doctor might be. Her mind returned to her article on Galveston historical homes. The physician gave her a tour, and she remembered his address on 63rd Street. "Well, thank you. Tell him Jennifer Harry was here," she said, handing the nurse her business card.

•   •   •

The cold moonlight shone through the torn plastic curtain, casting a sprig of harsh light across the dusty bedroom floor. It was a dream again. The room was small; the floor covered with toys and one special model airplane.

He burst through the door with a ghoulish look on his face. "Where are you, Lee Wiley," he said, unable to focus by this time? "Is that my plane? Didn't I tell you-awl not to play with that their plane?"

The boy stood up with a start. "Don't hit me again, Daddy!" It frightened the young boy with the dark brown hair, as he looked up at his Father towering over him. The man looked so tall and powerful. His stuffed animal Ben was at his side and he thought of blocking the blows but then realized his love for the Bear.

The man looked at the boy. He had tears in his blood- shot eyes, held a bottle of whisky by its neck in his right hand, a long black belt was in his left. "Lee Wiley., damn you, boy! I told yaw-all not to play with my airplane, look you put a f#in hole in the wing! Why do that, boy? You know yaw-all torment me, so much!"

"I wanted to fix it for you. It was there already, Daddy. Look I can fix it." The boy placed a piece of tissue paper over the whole frantically. He looked up at the man. "Don't you love me anymore, Daddy?"

With that, the man hit the boy with the belt across the back of his neck. It knocked him over, the plane landing overturned on the floor. The boy began to cry. It was not full out crying, but sobs held back out of bravery. It was not the first blow of the night, or of the boys' life, for bruises were continually covering his little back. The man took a long swig from the bottle. He wiped his mouth with his hand containing the belt. He picked up the plane, crushing the other wing. The man looked up at the boy with an accusatory stare. He shook his head negatively and walked away, slamming the boy's bedroom door.

The boy cried profusely. With his head down, sobs were let loose in buckets. He grabbed the bear and crawled into his tiny unmade bed, covering his head with a torn blue blanket. Bear decorated too small jammies, covered his growing legs. His little feet stuck out from under the cover, one foot with a sock, the other uncovered. He was cold and shivering.

Gradually the crying calmed down.

The blaring country music down the hall stopped as the 45 record ran out. The boy sat up, hugging his bear. He crawled out of the bed to the door, reaching up to the brass knob. Down the hall was his Father. He was passed out on the floor, the bottle in his hand. Vomitus encircled his mouth. The belt and the bottle were still in his hands. The boy dropped to his knees. He put a hand on the man's chest.

"Daddy, are yaw-all okay?"

The man groaned and rolled over. He pushed the child's hand away. The belt curled indignantly on the wooden floor.

. . .

No one answered the front door, but the girl was persistent seeing his doctor's Z-car parked in the driveway. Eventually the porch light came on, and the doctor peaked through the fissure. He wasn't sure of who she was, just awakening from the repetitive disturbing dream, and he looked at her in silence.

"It's Jennifer, Dr. Hickok!"

Lee W. thought for a moment. Eventually he shut the door, removed the chain, and then opened up for the girl. Standing in socks, the man was unshaven, his hair a mess. He was thinner than she remembered, and his hands trembled as he shook her hand. He had a healing abrasion on his forehead, dressed in a wife-beater shirt and jeans with a hole in the knee. "Come in, Ms. Harry," Lee W. said hardly above a whisper.

The house was a mess, turned over chairs, pillows cast about, and a large crushed dent graced the hall wall. Dishes stood in the sink with a vomit covered red-white-and blue cowboy boot. A hall lamp was ajar, its shade nowhere to be seen. It was dark inside, most lights extinguished. Lee W. sat slowly on the couch. Jennifer followed him, asking if she could sit by his side. Lee W. stared across the room silently. The man looked horrible. "I went to your office."

Lee W. looked quizzically at the girl. He shook his head affirmatively and whispered: "been sick."

"What's wrong, may I ask?"

Lee W. looked down. He picked at an invisible thread on his jeans, considering his answer.

Jennifer realized the private nature, but her journalistic instincts were flaring. She felt for the man, but she had work to do. A story about the Governor's death was at her fingertips and here sat the key to unraveling it. She asked again: "what's wrong, Dr. Hickok?"

Lee W. for the first time looked the reporter in the eye. "Stopped drinking!"

It all clicked in place. Lee W. had withdrawn from his alcohol addiction. His appearance matched that sorry state. "That's good," she said, feeling sympathy for the man. She too heard rumors as to his alcoholism.

"Ya, its best," Lee W. said, after which he looked away sadly.

"That's great Dr. Hickok! How do you feel?"

Lee W. looked at the girl and chuckled to himself. "Like shit. What do you think? What do you want?" For the first time, he seemed to recognize the mess in his house. "Look at this place. Even Amber has given up on me, I guess?"

"Well first, thanks for taking care of my Dad, you know Dupree? I phoned him this morning, and he says he feels better than in years. Is that possible?"

Lee W. shook his head yes, slowly, yes. Dupree Harry's prostate cancer was in remission after removal of the testicles. Miraculous improvement could be the result.

"Well, you did a fabulous job," Jennifer said sincerely. Lee W. said nothing, staring at the girl.

There was an uncomfortable silence that followed. Jennifer repositioned herself, replacing the couch pillow carelessly cast on the ground. "Dr. Hickok, we have to talk about that night. You know about the Governor."

"He died," he said with little emotion.

"Yes, but why?"

Lee W. spoke several sentences for the first time. "People just die from surgery. It's risky. Just medicine. No one has to be to blame."

"But the sequential compression boots were off. You know that Mr. Goldine removed them, don't you?"

It was clear that Lee W. knew. He looked down at his jeans again, picking at the invisible thread.

He looked up at the girl. She noticed for the first time his right eye, a red subconjunctival hemorrhage coloring his bloodshot sclera. This man's been through the mill, she thought to herself.

"PE's happen even with boots," he said, referring to a pulmonary embolism that killed the Governor.

"Yes, but Dr. Fields ordered them! Shouldn't they have been on?" Jennifer got a silent, weak confirmation by the slow nod of Lee W.'s head. "And should a layman be deciding about something as important as sequential compression boots?" Another weak confirmation with a nod. Silence followed. Lee W. lay back on the couch. He obviously felt horrible.

Jennifer sat quietly thinking about her Governor's article. She now had several confirmations that ordered sequential boots were not on at death. She received an anonymous nurse's note accusing Goldine of removing those boots against Dr.'s orders. She would have to dig up that nurse and get her on the record, but Dr. Hickok was the main informant.

"Dr. Hickok, I will let you lay down. I need to get going. Thanks for your care of my Dad." She pulled his legs onto the couch and gently placed a pillow under his head. Lee W. was asleep as she left.

. . .

Abbott Frankenstein moved to the cabinet television and turned the on-switch, the set as always tuned to KTRK Houston news. He then sat at his vast desk. The antacids he was drinking night and day had stopped working, but he swigged a mouthful, anyway. A young black reporter named Jennifer Harry appeared, her presentation especially relevant to the University President.

"Breaking news today on the death of J.T. Splintter, the former Texas Governor," the nicely dressed black woman reported. "Autopsy places the cause of death being a large pulmonary embolus, a deadly blood clot lodged in the lungs. The blood clot, termed a PE, caused a sudden death without a chance of recovery, despite exhaustive resuscitative maneuvers.

The autopsy, and eyewitnesses, indicate the absence of preventative sequential compression boots, devices the attending physician Dr. Mark Fields ordered for the Governor. These boots prevent the development of leg blood clots, the source of most PE's. They are standard in the post-abdominal surgery patients like the Governor. Katy Marquette registered nurse goes on record for KTRK."

A new scene is present. "Thank you for time Ms. Marquette," said Jennifer Harry to the Governor's nurse. The nurse shook her head in response nervously. "Ms. Marquette, you were the last nurse to attend the late Governor, is that correct?"

"Yes, I was the nurse on the morning shift. We had just given report before the event."

"Describe what happened."

"Well, I went from the room for a moment to get ice-chips. The alarm was sounding when I returned, and the Governor was on the floor and unresponsive. We coded him for the longest time, but... he... died!"

"Did the Governor wear sequential compression boots that morning?"

"No, they were taken off when I returned."

"Where were they?"

"Wadded up in his closet!"

"Who was responsible for taking the boots off?"

The nurse looked down for a moment. She then reluctantly answered. "Mr. Goldine was always taking them off."

"Do you think the Governor's Chief of Staff took them off that morning?"

"Yes, no question. The night nurse told me so."

"Why do you think he took the boots off?"

"They're hot and uncomfortable."

"Thank you for your time Ms. Marquette." The camera centered on her. "That is the story here at KTRK. Your source for Houston news."

Frankenstein moved to the TV and turned it off. He was smiling, unusual for the man. Schlomo Goldine was no friend of his. He remembered his attempt to legally take over the Governor's care with an advanced care directive. It did not apply to daily hospital orders, and the man could not write an order given his lack of hospital privileges. He returned to his desk and picked up the American Statesman newspaper folded nicely in his in-box. What he saw changed his mood for the worse.

The front page discussed the President's trip to Germany. As always, he turned to the health news page. Across the entire top of that page was the headline: **Drunken Surgeon responsible for Governor's Death?** Frankenstein gulped. His peptic condition turned for the worse. He skimmed quickly. They quoted the police-report on Lee W.'s arrest, his blood alcohol level, and the short timeline between surgery and the incident. They gave evidence that proved that level could only be obtained by intake of alcohol just before the surgery. They did not relate how Lee W.'s surgery stopped the bleeding, implying that he was responsible for the Governor's demise. They called for Hickok's resignation. Luckily, Frank Cercetti was not quoted. The reporter was a hack, Kegan Macintosh, well known from prior contacts.

Frankenstein sat back in his chair. He picked up the antacid bottle, which was empty, and tossed it in the trash. He then dialed the operator, asking to page Dr. Cercetti.

CHAPTER 18
Happy Days

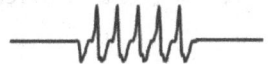

It was happy days for the chief of staff who practically skipped down the Austin capital hallway in a powder blue suit and a lime green Bolo tie. The storm passed, he was working again, and the sun shone outside beautifully. Singing birds should have accompanied the man. The marble floors hummed to the sound of his small cowboy boots, heals clicking and soles whistling. The Governor's death did not stop his business. Many politicians were vying for his services.

It was premature excitement and not to be, for down the hall stood Todd Franco with a scowl. "I have to talk to you, Mr. Goldine," Todd reported as Schlomo made his way into the office.

Happiness still ruled so without so much as a glare Schlomo responded. "What is it, my friend?"

Todd held up a black video tape, and said: "You have to see this!"

It was early in the evolution of television recording. No DVR or TiVo, no remote controller, no high definition recording. The state-of-the art was the Sony Betamax, and the political team surrounding the Governor dove into the technology.

"What is it," Schlomo quizzed?

Todd shook his head. "This is bad news. There could be real trouble. The damn media!"

The two moved quickly to a small room with a large television and a Betamax recorder. Schlomo threw his red striped briefcase on the floor, now not so happy. Todd struggled with the new technology, but eventually got an interference containing black screen.

"Get this going, Todd! I need you on this," Schlomo yelled. Soon a newscast was playing, the reporter discussing Reagan's trip to Europe. Then the screen moved to Jennifer Harry, the report shocking. She blamed the Governor's death on Schlomo. It correctly reported that he removed the boots. They even had an eyewitness, that nurse, Katy Marquette.

Schlomo was silent. His face fell downcast and dejected. A gloomy mood covered the room like a glove. The man turned from the TV set in disgust, and began stomping his small black boots like a drumroll, reminiscent of an immature child. His comb-over bounced up and down in disgust.

"Don't they know the Governor asked me to remove the boots? He wanted those blasted things off."

Schlomo thought for a moment. "The directive, I'll show them the directive!" Schlomo ran to his briefcase and removed the legal document. The Governor signed and notarized it before his death and placed all end-of-life decisions with Schlomo Goldine. Even Schlomo knew it did not apply to day to day orders, and he threw the document onto the floor, remembering that.

"Fax that worthless document to all the media." Schlomo paced. "He is a drunk. Don't they know that?" He referred to Lee W. Hickok. Schlomo repeated under his breath. *"A member of the surgical team was drunk that night.* McIntosh; where's his article?" He rushed out of the room to his office, grabbing his desk phone. Turning to a Rolodex he found the journalist's phone number.

The man answered on the first ring. "McIntosh," he responded.

"Where is that blasted article, you moron!"

"Who is this?... Goldine?"

Schlomo did not respond to his question. "Hickok, drunk... where is the article you ginger bag-pipe?"

"Well, I beg your pardon! Did you see today's American Statesman, fool?"

Schlomo thought and then slammed down the phone. "Todd," he said, turning to the assistant. "Where is that paper?"

Todd produced the tabloid. He turned to the health section headline. "Ya I was going to tell you!"

Schlomo grabbed the paper. He read silently. A wicked smile came over his face. He then read out loud. *"Drunken Surgeon Responsible for Governor's Death?* Of course he is!" Schlomo went on to read the entire article out loud. The article reported Hickok's DWI arrest and his blood alcohol level. It correctly reported that drinking of alcohol must have occurred before surgery. Schlomo's plan formed. A formal inquest by the state legislature here in Austin was in order. He could see the testimony now. The center of this Schlomo himself.

• • •

Lee W. awoke on the couch. The first thing he noticed, an absence of a pounding headache. Since his drinking binge, a blinding headache cursed him. It was finally gone, no throbbing pressure behind his right eye. He was stronger as well, bouncing up off the couch. He remembered the reporter, a nice girl, the daughter of his patient Dupree Harry. He righted the dining room chairs and replaced the shade from the lamp.

He made strong coffee in the kitchen. He poured steaming brew into a UTMB orange mug while whistling. Without thinking, he opened the cabinet over the coffeemaker. Then he remembered he did not drink anymore. A space beside stacked plates was present in the cabinet where the brandy used to always be. Lee W. remembered that the coffee actually tasted better without *freshening*. He was glad to be sober, standing here with no substance in his bloodstream. How many years had it been? The coffee was delicious.

He grabbed the beige wall phone and dialed from memory. She answered with some tentativeness. "What about breakfast, my Love?"

"Hi, how are you this morning?" Amber said with some worry in her voice.

"I feel good. My headache seems gone, I'm strong!"

"Breakfast, where?"

"Jill's, I'll pick you up." The diner was symbolic. The diner's owner, Jill, was Amber's friend from high school. The last visit was when he was a drunk.

"Okay," Amber said slowly.

A shower in the bottle cap containing bathroom, and Lee W. was in his car driving carefully to Amber's Condo. He recalled the storm called Patrice and was glad for the clear skies. He turned on the passenger seat heater for Amber's benefit, recalling how the switch had done him in with the police-man. All was well.

They parked on Seawall, Lee W. hurrying to open Amber's door. He noted the keyed in Superman still looking at him with accusations. They hugged, a long one for Amber, and a reassured one for Lee W. from Jill. He ordered, finished and enjoyed his usual this time. They even offered no brandy for the coffee. The grits were full of texture, with even a hint of some taste, as the world looked bright for the first time in years. Amber enjoyed her conversation with Jill. They spoke about the past and the future. Yes, life was outstanding for the couple, however life changes occur and often so quickly.

• • •

"We have an announcement concerning the death of Governor J.T. Splintter." Schlomo tapped the microphone as he spoke.

They were gathering in the Governor's mansion, microphone after microphone attached to the podium like penguins fighting for a fish, ready to broadcast the news conference. There was a hum of anticipation in the crowded room. The media were present in force. Newspaper reporters, local television personnel, and nationwide affiliates crowded into the small room. Kegan McIntosh took a seat at the back. The boss, Norman Coleman, and Jennifer Harry represented KTRK.

"We need to get going." Schlomo had again dressed in his lime-green suit with matching bolo tie. He was tapping his small booted foot, impatiently. The room slowly quieted down. "Governor J.T. Splintter of the great state of Texas was murdered in Galveston last week!"

The room was aghast with murmurs. Reporters everywhere stood and shouted. The security personnel moved to the crowd edges. A perfectly timed film ran showing the Governor walking under his own power into UTMB. Soon the hearse appeared. "The Governor's death was not due to natural causes, but rather a lack of routine accountability led to his untimely death. The alcoholic presence of Dr. Lee W. Hickok was well known in the Galveston community. Why then was he a member of the surgical team? This is unacceptable and reeks of culpability. I am astonished at the lack of responsibility at this University. Evidence shows that the Dr. was under the influence of alcohol at the time of surgery. His blood alcohol level, 19 minutes post-op of 0.18, implies an extreme level during the surgery. His presence in some way caused or influenced the subsequent expiration of the chief executive."

Schlomo stopped for a moment. The room was silent. "A legislative inquest is necessary. For once, your state senators need to move into action. I call on the new Governor, Warren Thornton, to insist these useless politicians investigate this crime."

Schlomo stood alongside the too-tall podium and relished the reaction in the room. Stone silence grew to a loud buzz. The audience threw questions out for the man.

"They hailed him a hero!"

"His presence was detrimental to the surgical team. This is obvious." Schlomo said proudly.

"But the Governor died of a blood clot."

"A minor event, the actual story is inappropriate vetting of a team member."

Norman Coleman handed copies of the anonymous documents delivered to KTRK to his budding reporter. She stood and waited for an opportunity to speak. "J.T. Splintter died of a pulmonary embolus directly because of the absence of sequential compression boots that you yourself removed, Mr. Goldine!"

The room was silent. The room turned its attention to the young reporter. Schlomo spit. "An irrelevant fact." He held up the advanced care directive. "You should all have received a copy of this last testament of the Governor on your fax machines. The Governor directed me to manage his care. I have a hand-written note from him directing me to remove those unnecessary discomforts. We must recognize the patient's wishes."

And so the debate continued. It is an age-old question of patient's rights versus medical wisdom. It cuts at the question of who is in charge in the hospital. The patient or the Dr's. Schlomo eventually left the podium. He re-emphasized the need for a senate inquest. They smeared Lee W.'s name. They forgot his surgical skills during the case. They threw common sense out the open wood trimmed windows of the room.

CHAPTER 19
The Judge of Galveston

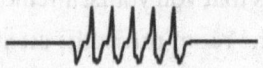

The Galveston county courthouse, or customhouse, was built in 1838 and rebuilt in 1861. It was a beautiful, classic-revival building; three stories of brick, white columns, and iron, the later incorporated into the building's foundation. It is this iron that allowed it to weather the 1900 Galveston hurricane, the country's worst natural disaster. The storm leveled the island, killing between 6 and 12 thousand individuals. Minor damage to the customhouse occurred. The building had an abundant history, including occupation by the Confederate army during the civil war. While soon to be a historical site, it functioned as the courthouse and post-office in 1983.

It was an overcast day when Andrew Calhoun met Lee W. at the courthouse. He was to be arraigned on the driving while intoxicated charges. The two met briefly off the courthouse steps to talk about the proceedings.

"The judge is hard, Lee W.! It's Johnnie, and he's often out of control. A prodigious drinker in his own right. I've seen him drinking on the bench. He'll give you a hard time, but sentence you probably to probation and driving restrictions on your license. Probation will be 3 to 10 months and is mandatory. Now he won't go lighter on you. He doesn't like medical doctors."

"Really? Why is that?"

"Rumor is that his daddy was a physician, and he hated his daddy. Whatever the cause, it just a fact, and we have to deal with it."

"Johnnie's at it again," Calhoun said, pointing to his right. Here sat a rusty VW bug parked by the mailbox, obstructing the path of the next vehicle. A large mud caked, white truck with lifted suspension, huge running lights on the cab, and a gun rack filled with several rifles pulled up behind the truck's occupant, and the driver lay on the horn. Calhoun and Lee W. moved close to see Jennifer Harry in a developing altercation with the infamous judge. The judge got out of his oversized truck, leaving it ajar on the street behind her. He knocked on the tiny VW driver's window smugly, demanding that the girl get out of the car. Jennifer obliged, moving to the street holding her leopard skin backpack.

"Get that rat-trap off the street before I write you!" The Judge was livid, standing in jeans, cowboy boots, and a white tee-shirt with a confederate flag stenciled on the front. He removed some paper from his jeans and wrote down her license plate, using the VW trunk as an easel.

"And who are you?" Jennifer set her pack on the ground. She was not intimidated by the shorter man, who was angry and spitting his words.

"I'm the Judge of Galveston!" The judge stood up to the woman. He announced his title to the world at the top of his voice. "Get that kraut car off the road woman!"

Jennifer was not smiling. The girl looked up at Lee W. and Calhoun with a frightened look on her face, recognizing Lee W.

Calhoun moved over to stand next to the Girl. "What trouble are you causing here Judge?"

"You," the Judge said! He seemed to remember the lawyer and some unpleasant fact. "Take your Sister away from here Calhoun!"

"She is not my sister, Judge!"

"I mean sister by kind! You are all alike!" The Judge kicked his off-road front tire in anger. He finished writing the license number and stuffed it in his back pocket. He turned and climbed into his truck. Skidding away, he flipped off the group.

Calhoun was hot. Lee W. moved to his side to calm the man. He introduced Calhoun to Jennifer.

Lee W., Andrew Calhoun, and Jennifer Harry stood in the street by the mailbox in silence. In every way, the Judge had insulted her. The group would remember the racial slur, sexist gesture, and the threat of a citation. However, Lee W. still needed to appear in front of the man.

Moving to her car, she said: "I have to go. I just needed to mail a letter! Really is there anything you can do about this man. I think he is mad!"

"I will work on it," said Calhoun.

The girl fired up the bug and drove away carefully.

They moved up the side-walk and climbed the stairs in silence. Calhoun was carrying a side-arm. He handed it to the guard, who returned it to the man after a superficial check.

While overcast, it was hot in the courthouse despite the open windows and several large electric fans mounted on poles. Perhaps the altercation had something to do with their body temperature. The two men sat in the courtroom. Calhoun removed a legal sized yellow tablet from his black briefcase. He dried his face and brow with a large rag from the case. He turned to Lee W. "You all right?"

Lee W. said he was fine. "What now?"

"Technically, we could not appear."

"Technically, I need to appear," Lee W. whispered.

The Bailiff stood, calling the court to order. "All rise, the honorable Judge John J. Olds is proceeding."

The man, now in a black robe, moved from a side-office and sat on the bench. He preceded to shuffle papers with an angry scowl. Lee W. knew he was in trouble. The Judge looked directly at him and drawled. "Call the first case."

The bailiff spoke. "The state versus Lee Wiley Hickok will be in session. The defendant will stand."

Lee W. stood. He tucked in his shirt, straightened his tie and buttoned one button of his Navy blue sports coat.

"What do you have to say for yourself?" The Judge was still angry, recognizing Lee W. from their recent altercation.

"Your honor," Calhoun said, taking the floor. "My client is a first-time offender of the Texas state drinking laws. He has quit drinking. He is registered in a state-approved rehabilitation program involving group sessions and random drug tests. Probation is indicated."

The Judge exploded. "Don't you ever tell me how to sentence councilor!"

"My apology your honor."

The Judge bent over the bench and glared at the two with hatred. "One year in the county jail, fifty-thousand dollars bail." With that he gaveled close the proceedings, turned around and disappeared into his chambers.

Lee W. and Calhoun were in silent shock. It happened so fast, there was nothing they could do. Lee W. sat down hard in the chair with a blank stare on his sweating face. Calhoun turned to him with a desperate look. He too sat hard in his seat next to Lee W.

"Here is the plan, Lee W.," Calhoun finally said. "Any reasonable person knows this is outlandish and over-burdening. I know the Mayor, and I will meet at my behest at least three of the five council members in the next few hours. They can't overturn his decision, but they can put weight on the man."

Lee W. looked doubtful. Willie Washington moved to his side, removing his handcuffs from his black polished belt. "Dr. Hickok, can I cuff and take you off now?" The man was sympathetic. He and others had experienced Johnnie's irrational behavior. Ironically, the man was a drunk, having served on the bench for twenty years.

Lee W. stood and placed his hands behind his back. He recalled the DWI and remembered the discomfort. The cuffs were in place and the officer led him off. Lee W. spoke to Calhoun as he just disappeared from the courthouse: "help me, Andrew." The door shut with authority and permanence.

.   .   .

That afternoon, officer Willie Washington had an unpleasant task to perform. He moved to his black and white Chevy Malibu squad car with reluctance. All officers were Judge Johnnie's whipping boy to some extent, but he was tiring of this. He read the address and made a U-turn on 21st Street. Jennifer Harry was at her dad's house on 7th. It was across the street from Mario's Flying Pizza in a two-floor shotgun house, built in the 40s and turned into a double-occupancy apartment. The first floor looked out over the front porch, the upper floor entered from a door to the right of the porch and up a flight of interior stairs. Washington opened the screen door and knocked quietly. Soon the girl appeared with a questioning expression.

"Ma'am, I beg your pardon, but Judge Johnnie is at it again. He has scheduled you for appearance in the courthouse next Monday at 8:30 AM. I am sorry, Ma'am! You must appear or be in contempt of court." Washington looked down. He turned slowly and walked away to his squad car.

Jennifer was frantic. She placed both hands overhead and cried dry tears. She grabbed the phonebook. It listed Calhoun under attorneys with a page ad describing his litigation skills. No one answered, but a message machine recorded by the man himself beeped away.

"Andrew, this is Jennifer Harry. You won't believe it. A police officer was just here. He insists that I appear in Judge Johnnie's court on Monday at 8:30 AM. What am I going to do? I'm due in Houston that morning, and besides, this is not fair. Call me!" She hung up the phone as her Dad walked into the kitchen. They embraced, the Father concerned for his daughter.

Jennifer just said: "you don't want to know Dad." She then briefly told the story of this morning and the officer's visit.

Frederick McCoy was the first phone call for Calhoun when he returned to his office. McCoy was the city's Mayor, elected in the fall election. He listened quickly to messages, repeating Jennifer's several times. The police officer's visit did not surprise him. He now had two issues to discuss with the man. Most important was his client's freedom. He had just witnessed a total abuse of power, a drunk judge gaveling an outrageous decision. Lee W. was a first-time offender. He had a perfect record. There was no public call for the man's prosecution, in fact he was a hero to many. He was an outstanding citizen in every way, a fine physician. The second issue was to quash Jennifer's appearance. The Judge was again abusing his power with the woman.

McCoy returned his phone call soon after lunch. They had met once before at a High School swimming meet. Both of their children were swimmers, competitors on opposing teams. Calhoun described the situation with Lee W.

"So Johnnie's at it again!" The man repeated the now famous moniker. "A year is a little stiff. Does he have the 50K?"

Calhoun put a stop to that. "If he did, I wouldn't recommend using it. That bail is outrageous. His sentence is a joke. Fred, can you do anything?"

There was a brief silence on the phone. "Well, we have a session tonight," he said, referring to that night's city council meeting. "You should speak to as many members as you can, Andrew. It would be so much better for them to hear this from you rather than me. You need to especially talk to J.D. Pike. He has the others in his pocket. Let me look here." A sound of a Rolodex was heard. "Yes, J.D.'s number is 556-2366." He then produced all members of the city council's phone numbers.

Over the next two hours Calhoun was able to speak to four of the council members concerning Lee W.'s case, speaking to an assistant of the fifth. All were understanding of the issue. All knew of Johnnie and his reputation. All were sympathetic. After discussing Jennifer with the Mayor and the council members, the decision was that Jennifer should not show up. The girl was cautious but thrilled to hear the news.

A phone call from Frederick McCoy the following morning settled Lee W.'s issue. They would release him from custody that day. He was to have a 10 month probationary interval. Here he was required to attend Diversion and submit random drug tests. A positive test would land him back in jail. He could drive only to and from his place of employment. The Judge recanted his appointment for Jennifer.

Amber picked Lee W. up at the county jail. It was quite a contrast to the other visit to the jail the night of the DWI. Lee W. was so happy to see the woman. He kissed her full on her lips. Lee W. took no chance. He insisted that Amber do the driving. As they pulled away from the police station, there were whoops of joy and thankfulness.

CHAPTER 20
Leave

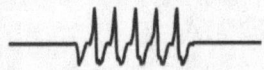

Hardwood flooring was planned for the floors of the Victorian. Galveston's Ball high school's gymnasium floor was being torn up, and Lee W. was the recipient of all that beautiful straight maple wood flooring. Answering a simple add in the *Galveston County Daily News* brought him the treasure trove, tied up and delivered to his front door for free.

He was not up to the task when drinking, but he felt wonderful for the first time in years. He needed to finish, given the weather in Galveston and the precious wood on his veranda. He cut the planks to length using an old Craftsman radial arm saw, set up on his porch. With canvas nail belt, his finish hammer given to him by his Dad that was older than himself, an old cracked tape measure, and 3-penny finish nails, Lee W. was on his way to finishing the project. He would measure two pieces at a time, note the length in ballpoint on his palm, select a matching plank, and trim the pieces to length with the electric saw. Soon progress and the end of the project were in sight.

The three o'clock KTRK news and a cup of Kroger coffee completed the day's work. His television was still a Black and White in an Old Danish modern cabinet from the 50's with rabbit ears. He turned on the set and waited as it warmed up. It took a moment to tune in to the broadcast and he just missed the segment on Reagan's Germany speech. "Mr. Gorbachev, tear *down this wall";* was seen across the bottom of the screen in white block letters. The newscaster appeared, finishing the piece.

"We turn now to a local segment. The death of Texas Governor J.T. Splintter at the University of Texas Medical Branch in Galveston has horrified the public. We have additional information on the case. Jennifer Harry has the story."

The story went on as before. It reported the pulmonary embolus and the absence of sequential compression boots. It detailed the removal of these and accused Schlomo Goldine for his part in the Governor's death. The story surprised Lee W., but he agreed with the story. The phone then rang, interrupting his concentration.

"Hello," Lee W. said.

"Dr. Hickok? This is Susie from Dr. Frankenstein's office. How are you?"

He was well and beginning to believe the good news on the newscast. "I am fine Susie, how are you?"

"Just fine Dr. Hickok. Dr. Frankenstein wants to schedule a meeting with you. What is your schedule like for tomorrow?" Lee W. thought about tomorrow. He was not due in the office until the afternoon, and he indicated he was free in the morning.

"How about ten AM then, Dr. Hickok?"

The urologist thought about the appointment for a moment. Something worried him, though Frankenstein had always treated him fairly. "Yes, ten AM would be fine, Susie." He placed the phone receiver on its hook gently thinking about the call. The news was done by the time he was off the phone, and he switched to a Houston Astros broadcast from the Astrodome.

.   .   .

Lee W. missed a week of work recovering from alcohol withdrawal. That morning, with excitement, he found himself eager to operate for the first time in years. He finally picked up the bottle caps from the tub, kept them in a drawer as a souvenir, showered and dressed for his AM Frankenstein appointment. He selected a white starched button down, grey silk tie, grey pressed slacks, grey tweed sports coat, and his black buffalo skin cowboy boots. In the early morning he washed the Z car, and except for the keyed door, found it that morning a beautiful shining, metallic green Datsun.

He arrived at Frankenstein's fifth floor office a few minutes early. Susie made a cup of tea, and he sat reading the newspaper; American Statesman. He read just the front page when Abbott Frankenstein ushered him into his beautiful office. The view that clear morning through his floor to ceiling window was breathtaking. Lee W. followed the man as he moved to his couch.

"I stopped drinking Abbott," Lee W. said quietly. Frankenstein smiled sincerely, silence reigning between the two physicians for a moment. "I heard a rumor to that effect. That is great for you, and the university Lee W. What happened?"

Lee W. thought back to the D.T.'s, and remained silent about his experience. "Sick," was his only response.

Frankenstein reached to a folded American Statesman on the coffee table. A knock interfered with this, Susie bringing a tea-set for their consumption. Returning to the paper, Frankenstein opened it to the Health section. The bold type said it all, and he pointed to McIntosh's headline.

Lee W. felt sick, temporarily. He left the paper open on the table, deciding not to read the article. He wasn't familiar with the author but felt immediate hate with a mixture of humiliation. Embarrassment mixed with a dose of self-loathing covered the man. He chose to drink that night, not anyone else. How could he have been so thoughtless, so cavalier, so carelessly taking life risking chances? He did so for years, but it caught up with him. Lee W. did not know what to say. He sat back on the couch and tried not to cry.

"They name you as the surgeon," Frankenstein said, taking the paper and placing it in a side-drawer on the edge of the coffee table out of view.

Lee W. spoke before thinking. "I... I... could offer my resignation!"

"You may have to, Lee W., but there is an option that I see."

Lee W. looked at the man with sad eyes. His sub-conjunctival hemorrhage was still visible. Suddenly he felt like an old man. He had not saved enough to retire. Images of foreclosure and Kellie's future played on his mind. He still had a good 20 years of surgical life. He fixed on the option the university president mentioned. "What option is there?"

"Well, you need that diversion. It is new in the state of Texas. In diversion, you remain licensed and practicing medicine in exchange for frequent drug tests and mandated group therapy. It is like AA for physicians, but mandatory if you are going to remain licensed. We leave the public out of the issue. In your case that newspaper article will complicate things, but when things die down, I think they will not harass you.

"Would you agree to this?" Frankenstein asked.

Any positive drug test would revoke the diversion. He could not fool the drug test people who were so experienced with drug seeking behavior. Sharing someone's urine would not be tolerated. Any controlled substance would be a violation, whether alcohol, cocaine, amphetamine, narcotic, sleeping pill or marijuana. The president was not familiar with another substance use in Lee W.'s case, but alcoholics used anything to get high. He waited for the man to respond.

Lee W. looked Frankenstein in the eyes. The urologist's eyes were sad, the hemorrhage unchanged. "That is what you talked about in the meeting. I will think about it, but yes, it seems to be an acceptable solution for me. Would I be able to operate?"

"Yes, as long as your license is intact through your successful ongoing completion of diversion. It would not affect your OR privileges. Do you use other substances?"

"I used cocaine once, just a snort. I have never really taken anything else."

"How about marijuana?"

"No, I took one puff in my life!"

"Because all substances are off limit. Cough medicine, even. Anything that is measured in a drug test."

"I have thought about it. I agree now," Abbott.

"No call me tomorrow. Do you have a clinic or surgery today?"

"Clinic."

"Okay," Frankenstein said, rising from the couch. "Well, call me on my private line in the morning, Lee W."

The two shook hands, and Lee W. walked out.

.   .   .

The dream dreamed on, as he stood tentatively on the cracked wet sidewalk, staring through old leaded glass windows stained from years of smoke. His beige Stetson hat cantered back on the top of his head, while a blue and white checkered shirt was pulled out partially at the waist with a black bolo tie standing ajar. He was wearing worn leather chaps tied loosely at the waist and covering stiff cowboy jeans worn over black buffalo hide boots. It was a worrisome decision to come to the place in the first place, and now that he was here he knew he would have trouble.

Lee W. tossed out a half-burnt cigarette, one that he almost never smoked, and entered the crowded bar, the door closing with a slam. No one noticed him, it was like he wasn't there, but he made his way across the room through a maze of packed people and sat at a very accustomed seat on the bar, just beyond its curve where the mirror ended and he couldn't see himself.

He removed his hat and set it carefully on the bar in front of him. The counter was made of cherry wood, scarred from extinguished butts, stained and blemished from its long history. He looked down and placed his booted feet on the iron rail before him, his chaps puckered at the waist from wear, a white rope the improvised belt. The room was stiff with smoke, loud with laughter and yelling, be he heard or felt no humor. Over all of it though, he could hear the jukebox playing the same tune as always, ZZ Top's Sharp Dressed Man.

He was anxious, this first visit since the event, but the loneliness of the room gave him some comfort and helped him forget what he was doing. He did not have to ask. It arrived before him; the bartender placing his drink and then disappearing, a tumbler with one finger of ice over what were two fingers of fine Kentucky Bourbon. It was loud in the room, but he could still hear the ice crack as the whiskey warmed them. And he knew that he could not resist.

He left his hat and drink and moved to the restroom across the room. He closed the red-painted door with its latch and turned to an old porcelain sink. The water was soothing as it ran, and he supported his weight on his elbows as he washed. His face was lit from behind by a single bare bulb which gave him a ghoulish appearance. Looking at himself in the cracked mirror it surprised him, for he wore an unexpected gold Christian Cross pierced earring in his left ear. He felt uncomfortable and removed the jewelry with his one dry hand, dropping it in his shirt pocket. The nerves were still there, growling ones telling him to leave. But he knew he couldn't resist.

He sat again at the bar, his hat and drink still unmoved. It called to him and he stared at the liquid as if it was his last chance. Looking around the bar, he realized where he was. It was different somehow, but the ambiance told him he was at Thirsty Thirties in Dallas again. The juke box played the same theme, and he tapped his toe to the beat. His hands were on the tumbler, his thumb flicking down a drop of moisture. He took a deep breath and through the smoke could smell the whiskey, that sweet smell that he had missed.

The tap on his shoulder was unexpected. Behind him, to the side, was what appeared as a made-up mannequin. She was much more than that, blonde curly hair to her shoulders, deep brown eyes, with a tight low cut green sweater and a black mini-dress. She wore black cowboy boots as well, and as the chair to right opened up she sat down.

"I would like a drink, yaw-all's seems to be going to waste," she said, staring Lee W. in the eyes.

Lee W. looked again at his glass, flicking another drop a moisture with his thumb. He picked up the drink and with it motioned to the bartender. "What are you drinking ma'am?"

The woman grinned at him with a beautiful, sad smile framed by red-painted lips. She wore thick make-up which covered just the beginning of an ageing face. "Seven N Seven would be lovely, sweet-heart!" The woman flicked her hair back with her left hand as she spoke, and her eyes flashed a forbidden gleam. She pulled a pack of Marlboro's out of her cleavage and looked for a light.

Lee W. was ready with his disposable lighter, taking an extra cigarette for himself. The woman's drink arrived, hers set down on a paper napkin. She took a small sip and puffed on her cigarette; the smoke causing her to fan it away from her eyes.

Lee W. was quiet, incapable of small talk.

"What are you drinking honey?" The woman said.

Lee W. handed his drink to the woman with a small smile.

She took it from him and sipped.

"Wow... that's nice." She placed her hand on his chaps again and lifted the drink to Lee W's mouth.

Memories of liquid entertainment flooded the man's mind. He took a small sip, the bite so memorable and pleasing to Lee W. It burned as it went down in a lovely manner, resting in the pit of his stomach like a jewel.

After that it was drink after drink, refill after refill, and the night became thick.

When the tune changed her affect picked up. She placed her hand on Lee W.'s chap covered leg and begged him to dance with her. He was reluctant but with the liquid encouragement, less so.

The two moved to the crowded dance floor, a wide swath of worn puck green linoleum not unlike the color of the old John Sealy's worn-out walls. KC and the Sunshine played a tune as the two danced a silly disco beat. Others crowded the dance floor, swigging long necks of Lone Star and Dixie, and smoking through the night. Songs merged into one, and then a change occurred. The juke box began playing Texas songs, and two step was what these two dancers were meant for. Cheers and yells of encouragement were heard as the floor became one long line. Late into the night, the music played until a slow tune began.

The two stopped and looked into each other's eyes. "How about a stop for more dancing in my car outside?" Lee W. said, pulling the woman to his side.

The woman grabbed Lee W.'s Bolo tie and pulled him to her lips. "No, but I will take a rain check on that!"

· · ·

He awoke on the silent water bed floating on his back, the sheets rounded into a disorganized ball at his side. His mouth was dry, his eyes tired, but his tongue was not cracked. He was dressed in shorts and a wife-beater shirt with two intact socks warming his feet. The ceiling fan beat circle after circle, the air drifting slowly. The device was out of balance and so made a dipping motion; the chain following the fan's center. The sun was just rising, a crisp shred of light just coming into the room through opened curtains.

He dosed on and off, but then woke with a start. Something in his dream's past warranting a retrieval. Thoughts of the night disturbed the man, and he set up bouncing on the mattress to the fan's beat. A hand went first to his left earlobe, the absence of the earing somehow pleasing the man. He crawled to the bed's side, sitting and thinking on the wooden frame. The nightstand drawer was empty, no cigarettes or plastic lighter. Jumping to his feet, he flung open his closet. Two black buffalo hide boots sat precisely on the floor. The blue and white checker shirt with the pearl white buttons all neatly fastened. He opened the shirt to reveal an empty pocket. In his dresser was a folded pair of leather Chaps, smooth without the slightest hint of wear. Behind them was a jewelry box, Christian cross earing sitting on black velvet. In the bathroom, he took a long look at his face. His eyes were white, no redness or new creases to report. Lee W. realized what did not happen that night, and it pleased him.

CHAPTER 21

Inquest

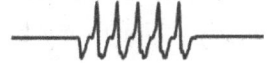

"The Senate will be in order," the chairman said, pounding the wooden gavel firmly. The Texas State Senate was in session in Austin the first day of February 1983. The media, senators, personnel, and witnesses were all in attendance, packing the small extension room on the south side of the capital. For a winter day, it was unusually hot, and multiple windows were open for fresh air. Carpets were laid to cover the miles of sound cables tossed on the aisle floors. Microphones littered various tables. Large television cameras were standing with technicians in the rear of the room.

"The Senate of the great state of Texas will be in session. Gentlemen, we convene to consider a serious subject. The death of our former leader Governor J.T. Splintter is the issue. I will read an opening statement," the elderly southern man said. "On January 6th, nineteen hundred and eighty three, the Governor of the State of Texas, J.T. Splintter expired in the facility known as UTMB, the University of Texas Medical Branch in the city of Galveston, Texas. His death is the subject of this inquest. On December 31, 1982, said officer of the state of Texas underwent abdominal surgery. He was attended by Dr.s Mark Fields, Nelson, Cromartie, and Hickok, and various medical personnel. We meet here today to review these events, for maleficence has been suggested. Senator, you may call your first witness."

"We call Dr. Mark Fields."

As with all the witnesses, Dr. Fields was sworn in on a Bible and asked to tell the truth.

"Dr. Fields, state your name and age for the record."

"Dr. Mark Malcolm Fields, 48 years old."

"Dr. were you the attending physician in December, attending to the medical and surgical care of J.T. Splintter?"

Fields went on to describe his involvement in the Governor's care. He briefly described the surgery and his role. Bleeding, the surgery, and Lee W.'s consultation were all discussed.

"Are you familiar with Dr. Hickok's work in the past?"

"Yes, we have both been on staff at UTMB for several years."

"To your knowledge was Dr. Hickok under the influence of alcohol during this surgery?"

There was an extended pause where Fields looked down at the long table. He shifted the microphone nervously. "Not to my knowledge, Senator," he said, emphasizing my knowledge.

The Senator looked at Fields suspiciously. He fingered his bushy brown mustache. There was a murmur in the room. He thought long and hard, but finished his questioning with: "I have no further questions for this witness."

The chairman reminded Fields that he was still under oath and subject to further examination. The next witness was Dr. Luis Gomez, the pathologist. He testified to his autopsy findings including the cause of death as a large saddle type pulmonary embolus. The origin of the blood clot was said to be the deep veins of the legs. Another Senator asked about the prophylactic use of sequential compression boots. Dr. Gomez commented briefly on their use and to a direct question indicated that they were not on the Governor.

Dr.'s Nelson and Cromartie, both anesthesiologists that night, testified to Hickok's character and surgical expertise. One was aware of his drinking reputation, but both did not detect any deficiency in his surgical skills.

They then called expert witnesses. Dr. Robert Withem from Mayo Clinic Rochester Minnesota testified about the use of sequential compression boots. He was an advocate and presented data that supported their effectiveness. Dr. Marcus Clay, from Massachusetts General in Boston, was not so supportive. He indicated that the literature was not clear on the subject. Some studies report important prevention of thrombotic events, while other's report no improvement. These controversies were like so many areas of medicine, equivocal.

They took a brief lunch break. Schlomo Goldine arrived with a large entourage. Lee W. Hickok arrived by himself and sat quietly in the back of the room.

They called the urologist to testify after the break. "State your name and age for the proceedings."

"Lee Wiley Hickok, 43 years old."

"Dr. Hickok, where were you on the night of December 31, 1982?"

Lee W. thought for a moment. "I was in my office, I had fallen asleep. Then Dr. Fields paged me for a consultation in room two of the operating room."

"What did you find in Dr. Field's operating room?"

"I scrubbed in to the case after reviewing the patient's CAT scan."

"Excuse me. Was the patient J.T. Splintter the Governor?"

"I did not know at the time, but yes eventually it came to my attention that we were operating on the Governor."

"Go on. What did you find?"

"Well, the left renal vein was dilated on the CAT scan, so I thought it was blocked to some degree by the patient's pseudo-cyst. I scrubbed in and noted extensive bleeding coming from that area. I was able to identify it and control the bleeding."

"Were you drinking alcohol or under the influence of any controlled substances at the time?"

A quiet growl went up from the audience. Lee W. kept eye contact with the Senator. He waited a good while, considering his answer. "Yes... Senator... I was drunk. Alcohol, I was using alcohol. I was drinking in my office."

The roar grew louder in the room. Photographers moved to the front, cameras snapped and flashes flashed.

"Is this your practice, Dr.?" The Senator asked with irritation. Lee W. looked down at the floor. He repositioned and smoothed his tie. Looking up into the Senator's eyes, he said quietly: "Yes."

"Are you an alcoholic?"

There was no pause, Lee W. said louder: "Yes I am an alcoholic."

"How did the alcohol affect your surgery?"

"As far as I know it didn't. I have drank for years, and I didn't really know the difference until recently."

The Senator gave up his questioning. Another continued. "What are you going to do about your addiction, Dr. Hickok?" Lee W. shook his head slowly. He was careful with his answer. "I have stopped drinking. I enter a diversion program next week. I can't drink again," he said with sincerity.

"I think the issue here is the pulmonary embolus," another Senator said taking the floor. "Yes, Dr. Hickok you are under oath and subject to reexamination. You are dismissed, please stay in the room, however."

Katy Marquette, RN. was called to testify before the committee. The woman looked horrified, walking slowly to the front, raising her tremulous hand and swearing to tell the truth on the Bible. She testified to the facts surrounding her nursing role. They discussed the sequential compression boots, their presence in the closet, and Goldine's guilt in removing them.

Schlomo stood and moved out of the room with an air of disgust. The proceedings were interrupted for a moment as he huffed his way out of the hearing.

There was a break at this point where the chairman formulated his closing summation. When he returned, the room was even more packed. "Let me say that the death of the Governor is a tragedy of epic proportions. He was my friend, and the State's proponent. Life is fragile however, and events such as these happen. In the Governor's case, the prevention of pulmonary embolus appears controversial. It is my understanding that these events happen even with sequential compression boots. The issue however, is who is in charge of the patient. The attending physician is legally charged with the patient's care. In this case that physician ordered the placement of sequential compression boots. It is not for this body to judge their use, but rather to support that physician. This body will issue a reprimand to Schlomo Goldine in this manner. Little enforcement is possible, but in our report he will be admonished."

"Now I turn to the issue of substance abuse in the operating room. Lee W. Hickok admits to being under the influence of alcohol at the time of surgery. From all testimony, his judgment or skills were not affected. The Governor's death apparently had nothing at all to do with Dr. Hickok's addiction. This is not to condone such practices. We all are under the supposition that our Dr.'s have clear, unaffected abilities. Lee W. Hickok took a huge chance that night and violated his Hippocratic Oath in doing so. This body reprimands him as well. It stipulates and supports his medical license with the caveat of completion of a diversion program and spontaneous drug tests for the period of two years. During that time, pending successful cooperation in the Diversion program, the State of Texas will allow him operating and clinical privileges at the University of Texas Medical Branch." With that the session was closed.

Lee W. was happy. Behind him sat Jennifer Harry quietly. She reached over the man's shoulder and shook his hand gently. Norm Coleman sat next to the girl. He too congratulated Lee W. One man who was not happy was Kegan McIntosh. The man stood and left the room quickly

Abbott Frankenstein had somehow concealed his huge frame in the room, or perhaps it was the tension that blinded Lee W. to his presence. For whatever reason, the urologist was unaware of the President's presence in the room that day. Lee W. stood and stretched his thin frame. He was pleasantly surprised by the inquest's findings, his presence in diversion already planned. Frankenstein tapped Lee W. on the shoulder. He turned and looked up at the man. A sincere smile covered the man's face, and the two shook hands in earnest. Frankenstein handed the man a manila envelope. Inside were the UTMB documents which led the media to Goldine. They were all marked for the mail. Lee W. did not understand. Jennifer Harry pointed to the UTMB logo. She explained the anonymous and key nature, realizing now that Frankenstein was responsible. All the pleased participants left the hearing in mass. They agreed to a dry lunch in town.

• • •

Goldine left his office in a huff. The Senate's reprimand would not stop him he vowed. He phoned his chauffer and arranged to be picked up outside. The same fellow who drove him from the hospital was there and he held the door open for the man. Schlomo had dreamed about a *Piece of Dream* since their last CB connection. He handed the address to the chauffer. He did not notice that the man did not read it. Darkness was coming over the streets. The driver wound his way through the back alleys of Austin. He parked the long limo in a particularly foul neighborhood and moved to open Schlomo's door.

Schlomo found the front door open, and he cautiously moved into a rundown flop of a house on a dirty alleyway. The room was pitch dark, and Schlomo walked across the room to where he thought he heard a sound.

Flash... flash... The camera cycled through multiple frames, catching Schlomo in the flophouse. A provocatively dressed woman was sitting on the broken-down couch. Schlomo tripped and fell with his face in her lap. Flash... Flash continued. The woman pushed Schlomo away, grabbing and removing a wad of his precious hair. He rolled onto the top of a low table; the camera capturing Schlomo's face and a large pile of cocaine. The chauffer took several other compromised photos. He grabbed his former boss by the buttocks and threw him out of the house on his face. The media would soon have a field day with the photos.

CHAPTER 22
Diversion

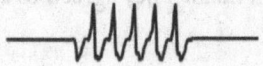

"Hey, let's get going people!" Jerry was pouring one of his many daily cups of coffee into a stained Styrofoam cup. He was a social worker and leader of the south Houston diversion group. "We have a new member today, group," he said enthusiastically. Ten individuals, seven men and three women sat at a long scratched mahogany table with folding metal chairs. They were all physicians or other health care professionals. These individuals could have been anyone from their appearance, but the group had drugs and alcohol in common. Jerry asked for some quiet while they sat looking at the newcomer.

"Group, we have a new member this morning," he said like an elementary teacher calling roll.

Lee W. squirmed in his chair, trying to smile nicely. He spoke quite often in front of people, but this was an unfamiliar experience.

Jerry was all business. He was silent and looked at the urologist with a serious questioning look. "Group, this is Lee W. Hickok. I believe you go by Lee W, is that right?"

Suddenly it was hot in the formerly cool room. "Yes," Lee W. responded. It was a shock to be sitting here and more so asked to speak first. Lee W. wished that he had read the brochure carefully, wondering what information he should share with the group.

"Well, introduce yourself Lee W."

Somewhere in his mind he recalled seeing similar meetings, where all the members would stand individually and announce that they were an alcoholic. He decided to remain sitting and not announce his addiction for the world to see. "I am Lee W. Hickok. I am 43 years old from Katy, Texas. I went to med school at Southwestern and did my residency at UTMB. I practice there, general urology."

He looked at the leader, hoping for a break. He felt sweat forming on the tip of his nose.

Jerry blinked, giving the new-comer a break. He shook his head affirmatively and turned to another on his right. "What about your urine, Thomas?" Here he referred to a slightly overweight man in a light blue Izod shirt.

The man grimaced and said just: "OH?"

"Yes, I know about it from this morning, Thomas!" Jerry looked at the man out of the corner of his eye. "What possibly could have kept you from your sample? You get here, you get to the lab, right!"

"I got up late."

"Unacceptable, never acceptable, but this is your second time in a year." Jerry had an incredible memory for facts. He was no nonsense, Lee W. would come to find out.

"You were late last week, you are just goofy, Thomas!"

Thomas was a gastroenterologist at Baylor. He was a cocaine addict who had failed rehab several times. His late appearance for group and failure to obtain a drug test were symptomatic of relapse. "I will not tolerate this. No medical practice until two sequential negative urines. That is without pay as you know."

Thomas turned away. He looked like a caught child. "I've got alimony!"

"I've got a violin!" Jerry mimicked the playing of the stringed instrument.

The group was uncomfortable. Everyone knew some fact in their own life that violated the diversion mandate. One stood to distract herself, turning on a lamp, one went to the restroom.

"Janet, why don't you introduce yourself for the group and Lee W. in particular?"

Janet sat as she spoke. She was a spray blond haired woman with beautiful painted red nails, a large bust, and a lively persona. "I am Janet Kawzinski... I am an alcoholic," she said quietly. "I am a psychiatrist, originally from New York. I have not had a drink in seventy-five weeks. I don't think your goofy Thomas," she said seductively. "No, I am here to just pee in a cup, I do so, but I could leave practice Jerry." There was a spark of anger towards the leader in the woman, why was not clear to the newcomer.

"Why did you come to Texas," said Si laughing. "Tell Lee about your drink of choice."

Janet shook her head negatively. She, unlike Si and others, was not laughing. "Liberal liquor laws. You know Si, Listerine is my drug of choice!"

Lee W. said out loud. "What, mouthwash?"

Si was hysterical. "Craziest thing I've ever heard. Psychiatry for the psychotic, Bombshell! Listerine contains the highest alcohol content of all the mouthwashes."

Janet stared at the man, and then at Jerry. "We've heard my story enough," she said tersely.

Jerry asked Robert to share. Robert had an obvious tremor, side-effect from his multiple years of drug usage. He was an old timer and had not failed a test in years. He was a pharmacist who used his proximity to narcotics, amphetamines, barbiturates, and benzodiazepines to his benefit, or to his detriment some would say. Robert began with the usual diatribe. "Hello, I'm Robert. I am a drug addict, I have been sober for six years, two months, and three days. Oh ya, I'm sixty-two years old. My grandson came to visit last week," He said slowly concentrating on the table before him. "I couldn't color between the lines because of my tremor." He continued looking down sadly. "I guess it is all right. He'll stop coloring soon."

Silence followed uncomfortably. Several sipped coffee to distract themselves. A siren howled outside, reminding all of their vulnerability.

"Si, introduce yourself, and remember to mention what you are accused of!"

Si was suddenly silent. He claimed to not use substances, quite a change for the group. He was a registered sex offender, however, and had a twisted story to match, all of which he denied. "I shouldn't be here. I am not an alcoholic or drug user like yaw-all. I made the mistake of dating a patient. I'm a gynecologist, and for some that is a rule breaker."

"Dating was not the issue Si," Jerry said standing to pour more coffee.

Si sat unhappily. He said nothing more.

"Si is accused of groping, and inserting, let's say his manly object, into a female's vagina during a pelvic exam. This occurred with multiple women, their stories all very similar. Oh, by the way, one girl was 13 years old."

A grotesque silence hung over the group. Lee W. wanted to leave. Suddenly the man's countenance appeared revolting and repulsive. The act evidently happened over many years. Some say that his first victim was in medical school.

"Well, a friendly conversation this morning. Anyone else want to speak?" The silence continued. All sat frozen at the table. Jerry stood and offered coffee. There were no takers.

"Well we meet, as you all know, promptly at 8:00 AM Wednesday. Do not be late, do not miss a sample. Be ready to tell us your true story Lee W!"

And so the diversion meeting was history, a friendly and pleasant gathering of willing professionals. Modeled after alcoholics anonymous. There was one big difference. While those at AA meetings, in general, want to be there, those at diversion were forced to attend, that is, if they were to keep medical licenses. It was an important distinction. The collection of mankind was no different from a typical AA meeting, however, where man's depravity was on display.

CHAPTER 23
Church

—/\/\/\/\—

The choir rocked with an amazing sound that fine Sunday morning. The parishioners stood in unison, as the hymn blasted their voices and their spirits to the cathedral roof on its way to worshiping God. The African Methodist Episcopal Church of Galveston was on fire for the Lord when the Hickok couple accompanied by regulars, Jennifer and Dupree Harry, the latter requiring some assistance, arrived and stood by their usual seats; hand waxed blackened oak pews, where sitting was not an option. There was a drummer who struck a beat, two twin ladies decorated in identical hairdo's and gowns banging matching facing pianos, and a sweet stringed section tuned to the Father's crystal clear divine note.

Lee W. was overwhelmed by the noise and excitement, as well over two hundred members stood jumping and lifting hands to worship the King, Jesus Christ. He was a Christmas and Easter church attender as a child, his parents dropping him off at a small Methodist sanctuary back home for the holiday services. He believed in God, just did not know Him. Amber believed and was thrilled to have her new fiancé in the loudest, largest Christian gathering on the island.

They dressed the choir in the finest golden gowns finished with exquisite ruby colored silk satin. The singers, men and women, held hands as they sang to the Lord. The audience was dressed for a blessed Sunday. Beautiful dresses with fine matching hats crowned with beautiful tulle, and men in their best suits filled the pews. When the choir finished everyone walked around, shaking friendly hands and hugging their enthusiastic neighbors, as kids ran the aisles.

A brightly dressed member moved to the podium to deliver the weekly announcements. He wore a maroon Nehru shirt, large gold cross necklace with pressed black slacks and spit polished matching maroon shoes. Clapping and joyful praise punctuated his every sentence about meals, charity, and love offerings.

When he introduced Pastor White, the young minister in a crisp black suit moved to the gold layered podium with a huge, friendly smile.

"Can I get an amen for our unmatchable Jesus choir!" The man spoke quietly but with a humble tone.

"Amen," echoed from the pews.

"And Pastor Hayes, I love you brother," the minister said referring to the announcement toting gentleman who raised his hand in response from the pews. The Pastor just stepped back and smiled at everyone in the congregation. "I see Brother Harry who stepped from the Lord's presence, just for the moment I remind everyone."

Dupree Harry knew that his wonderful daughter had dropped a note to the busy Pastor. He shook his head and smiled, placing a grateful hand on her shoulder. Yes, he would be in the Lord's presence soon enough, but was thankful to be present on earth, if only for a short while. Lee W. reached along the pew and rubbed his patient on the knee.

"I have a message this morning for my Brother's and Sister's in Christ. It is the message of our time. It is the solution to our condition. For you-see, this is a troubled and wretched land, is it not? Man is disturbed and lost. He is missing, mislaid, and miserable. For he is lost and not saved." The Pastor moved from the podium and stared at his congregation. He was a powerful black man who was dead serious but one with love in his eyes. He had a smile that melted the arrogant mind. "We are born separated from a loving God, are we not? But there is Good News!"

The congregation agreed with the Pastor. It is like they knew the loving ending. Amen Brother was heard, many lifting their hands to the sky.

"You know that God so loved us. Yes, he loved us before we loved him back. *He so loved us, that he gave his only begotten Son.*" The Pastor paused for effect, letting that wonderful news sink in. "His only Son! I have just one son myself. I know what that means. You know that he has gone to be with the Savior." Pastor White's only son had died in infancy. "But I wouldn't give him up, if I had a choice. I am a selfish man. I loved him and think of him daily. But the Lord knows better. And so the sacrifice, God gave his only Son, now that's a miracle! *That who so ever believes in him shall have eternal life.* Now we are talking. Life eternal. Not just here in Galveston. Not just here in Texas, not just in the world, no in heaven and for eternity."

The Pastor returned to the podium. He picked up a small, worn Bible. "John 3:16 is the foundation of our life. Now how long is eternity? It is not a year, it is forever. It is not a decade, it is forever. Eternity means endless, forever."

He moved again to the podium's side, wiping his brow with a gold silk handkerchief. "Now how do I get this, this wonderful all powerful, overpowering gift?" He paused for effect. "It is free," he whispered. "What? He shouted: IT IS FREE," the man screamed.

The audience went crazy. Cheers and clapping filled the massive room. Hallelujahs and amens were shouted out. Formerly quiet kids danced in the aisles to their parents' chagrin. The choir reassembled quietly.

He wiped his brow for a second time. "You only have to ask him. You must do this publically. Jesus said: Whoever acknowledges me before others, I will also acknowledge before *my Father in heaven.* (Matthew 10:32) You want to be acknowledged before God, am I right?"

"Amen Brother," was heard from every end of the building.

The choir started playing a quiet hymn.

The Pastor stepped down to the Sanctuary floor. He smiled brightly. "I will give you a chance to acknowledge God this morning. If you have never asked the Lord Jesus Christ to enter your heart and grant you the gift of eternal life, you need to come this morning and ask the Savior into your heart. Now, no one can do this for you. It is your job alone. It is the only time in your life that you will need to do this. It lasts forever. No for eternity. Now you come."

The band played quietly, while the choir sang. The parishioners were on fire. Those that came gave their lives to the Lord or rededicated their lives in Jesus. The sanctuary floor was full of believers. Some were crying, some on their knees, others raising hands to God.

Lee W. had felt a burn in his heart, really, from the moment he entered the cathedral. It had built through the sermon, but now he was ready. He knew that the Pastor was talking to him. Tears built up in his eyes and he let them flow. He knew that he was wretched without this. It was new to the man. He watched others before him carefully. Taking a step out of the pew, he walked slowly to the front. He was surprised, not feeling at all uncomfortable. He was not ashamed, only humbled by the glorious opportunity.

At the front he hugged the Pastor and shook his hand excitedly. The Minister whispered in his ear. "There was an air of expectation in your face. I saw it, Brother." Before he knew it he was on his knees, his cowboy booted soles visible to the world as his soul was saved.

Amber was next to him the following moment. She rededicated her life as well. She kissed Lee W. on the cheek and held his hand in the air.

Their wedding the next month was in the African Methodist Episcopal Church. Amber shone like an Angel from Heaven, her hair curly and flowing to her shoulder. She wore a beautiful pink dress embroidered in white, and carried an enormous bouquet of flowers. A brief ceremony performed by Pastor White, complete with the choir singing *Amazing Grace*, re-married the loving couple. Kellie, their daughter, carried the ring that Lee W. had originally given to Amber. She was a beautiful young woman and so happy for her parents. And the Angels rejoiced in Heaven.

CHAPTER 24
The End

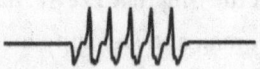

The old porcelain scrub sink purred with happiness that morning. It was the first case and hence the best of the day, and Lee W. was happy. The iodine soap lather flowed from his hands like a bee's finest honey. Dripping and collecting in the sink's bottom, the scrubbing and antiseptic left his hands a glistening brown. Overhead music played what he imagined as a hymn from church, and he hummed, excited for his new life. Lee W. shook his hands free of water and moved to OR room two's swinging door. Holding his hands up for sterility, he turned and backed through the entry. The room was buzzing with action; the patient draped in green. Brilliant white lights focused on the task, anesthesia concentrating at the table's head, the scrub nurse hovering over her mountain of shiny stainless instruments. All were present for Lee W.'s and the patient's purpose and need. As he entered the room a feeling of pride and yes some power overwhelmed the sober urologist, for once not needing the liquid sweet amber.

ABOUT THE AUTHOR

William Lynes, MD is a 66-year-old (b 1953) retired Stanford trained physician, urologist, award winning author, and speaker on physician burnout. His first novel is *Pirates, Scoundrels and Kings*, a fantasy/adventure work of fiction. Subsequent medical genre fiction works include the award winning *A Surgeon's Knot, Luger Rounds, 606 University, The Plumber* and *Huntsville.* His most recent work is *Sweet Amber.* He is the father of three grown sons and lives with his wife Patrice in Temecula, California. http://lynesonline.com

NOTE FROM THE AUTHOR

Word-of-mouth is crucial for any author to succeed. If you enjoyed *Sweet Amber*, please leave a review online—anywhere you are able. Even if it's just a sentence or two. It would make all the difference and would be very much appreciated.

Thanks!
William Lynes

Thank you so much for reading one of William Lynes's novels.
If you enjoyed the experience, please check out our recommended
title for your next great read!

A Surgeon's Knot by William Lynes

The winner of the Pencraft Award

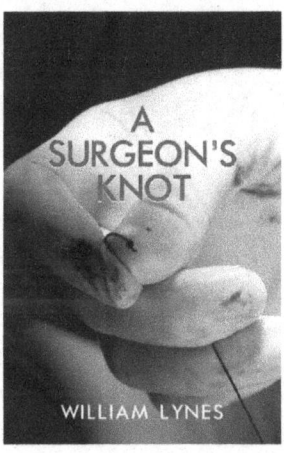

"Heart-pounding tales of a surgical intern that are both
terrifying and profound. This medical thriller will stay with you
long past the final chapter."
–BEST THRILLERS